Apple Tree

A Novel by

Derrick Harper

Self Made Publishing
TARBORO, NC

Apple Tree
A Novel By Derrick Harper

Copyright © 2015 by Derrick Harper

All rights reserved. No part of this book may be used or reproduced in any form or by any means without the express written permission of the Author except for the use of brief quotations in a book review.

This novel is a work of fiction. Any resemblances to actual events, real people, living or deceased, organizations, establishments or locals are products of the author's imagination. Other names, characters, places and incidents are used fictitiously.

Apple Tree/ Derrick Harper. -- 1st ed.

ISBN 978-0692470923

Dedication

Dedicated to my family, friends, supporters, and to all seekers of light and truth

Introduction

My name is Arkeba Kenyatta Towns, I'm 21 years old, 5'7", 135 pounds, about two shades from being called white, with long straight hair that hangs down my back. I was born and raised in Tarboro, North Carolina, in a neighborhood called East Tarboro. Before this revelation starts, I gotta tell y'all, some of the nastiest, freakiest, and most deadly stuff happens in the country. As this story unfolds, I want y'all to understand, I tried to do right, but the apple didn't fall too far from the tree.

Chapter 1

1989

Cassandra Towns

I walked down Bradley Avenue in my black biker shorts, making my plump ass jiggle with each step. Men rode past me calling my name, blowing their horn, but I paid them no mind. I only cared about the money, and I felt that a black man's money wasn't long enough for me to put my legs in the air.

The sun beamed down on me as I walked to the jewelry store downtown to meet the jeweler before his wife showed up at 3:00. The cool air ambushed my body as I entered. My mind traveled to how Chuck had rammed his tongue up my ass the last time. My asshole had always been off limits, but this white man knew his dick wouldn't do the job for me. Chuck was in his mid-thirties, a little over six feet, with broad shoulders. He was white as snow, and his black hair offset his baby blue eyes. The motherfucker was fine, with a six-inch dick that was round like my middle finger. That fucker could lick the hell out of some pussy, though. I don't know if I was more in love with his tongue or his money. Either way, they both got me wet. Even though my mother raised me right and made me finish school, I couldn't care less about that shit! I'm stacking my money so I can buy my own house and car.

Chuck walked past me and put the closed sign up. I could smell his expensive cologne as he moved around me. I didn't know anything about being freaky. I had only been with four white men, and I let them do freaky stuff to me for that paper. Yes, I lost my virginity to a white man! So what? I bet y'all bitches lost y'all shit for free! The motherfucker gave me $5,000 for my sixteen-year-old virgin pussy. Damn right, he can get it! Shit, the black men didn't really have that kind of money around my area. If he did, he sold drugs, and how long would that last before his stupid ass got killed or put in jail? These crackers gonna pay me for taking my ancestors' pussy during the time of slavery. Anyway, back to Chuck and me...

Chuck walked up to me and tongued me down. I hated when he did that shit! His mouth stayed so damn wet! It didn't stop my pussy from jumping, though. I don't know what the fuck came over Chuck, but as he kissed me, he reached into the back of my biker shorts and pulled my ass cheeks apart. I could feel the sweat from my walk run down my crack. Chuck then rubbed his finger down the crack of my ass, over my asshole. I jerked away fast. We had not spoken a word to each other, and this fucker done stuck his hand down the back of my shorts, touching my asshole! I was so embarrassed. I know his hand smelled like shit.

"Stop, Chuck, don't do that shit!" I said, pushing him away.

"Come on, Case, it's just a part of sex!" Chuck said as his dick begged for release from his tight Wrangler jeans.

"I've never done that, and my ass is made for shit coming out, not going in!"

Chuck grabbed my arm and pulled me into the back room.

"No, Chuck, you will not smell this until you give me the money that you promised me!" I said, pulling away.

"I'll triple it if you let me do anything I want to your body," Chuck said.

I thought hard about that. Shit, Chuck already was gonna give me a thousand. That would be three thousand. I pushed Chuck in his chest.

"You don't love me. All you want is my body!" I faked like I was about to cry.

"You know our agreement, but I do love you. I just can't leave my wife."

"So what do I have to do?"

"Let's start from here and let things take its course," he said and pulled me into the room.

Shit, for three thousand dollars, I was out of them biker shorts and halter top in thirty seconds. Chuck stepped out of his jeans; his ass cheeks were whiter than the rest of his body. I walked up behind him and slapped him on his ass as hard as I could.

"God damn it, Case, don't do that shit!"

I laughed. His face and ass had turned bright red.

"I'm sorry, baby. How can I make it up to you?"

I grabbed his dick and rubbed back and forth.

"It's so big, how will you get that in me?"

I tried so hard not to laugh. Chuck placed his hand on top of my head and lightly pushed me down to my knees. I knew he wanted his dick sucked. I had never sucked dick; I left that to the white girls. My pussy too damned good to be doing extra shit. I took hold of his dick and smelled it. I almost gagged, just from smelling the precum.

"Do I have to, baby?" I whined.

"If you want the money, or you could give me the other hole." He looked down at me and smirked.

I thought real hard about that then stood up, bent over, and looked back at Chuck's dick. I was so scared. It looked like it had grown in width and length. Chuck pushed his dick into my wet pussy. After coating his dick with my juices, he started pulling it out. I screamed like he was killing my pussy, hoping that he would leave it in there. Chuck took two more pumps. I pushed my ass back to him, screaming as loud as I could, even though he wasn't doing shit. I just didn't want him fucking with my ass. He pulled out of my pussy and I dropped to the couch like he had ripped my pussy apart.

"Come on, Case, bend back over," Chuck said.

"Can we think of something else? I haven't cum yet."

"I tell you what, baby, to show you my love, I'll give you the three thousand and let you pick out any ring you want that's under seventy-five hundred."

I gave Chuck the biggest smile I've ever had. I stood up, turned around, and bent all the way over the couch. Chuck leveled his dick at my ass entrance and worked his dick head into my asshole. It felt like a golf ball had popped in my ass!

"No, Chuck, wait baby …wait!" I said quickly.

Chuck gritted his teeth at the tightness and pushed the rest of his dick in. It felt like I had to shit so bad! I screamed my ass off. After Chuck stroked me a couple of times, the pain somewhat went away and I could feel my ass getting wet. The craziest thing happened! I felt myself about to cum out of my ass! The nut felt so different! Chuck slapped my ass hard, scaring the shit out of me and making me lose focus. He mumbled something, and then came in my ass, dropping his drool on the back of my neck.

Chuck pulled out of my ass and walked off to the bathroom. I lay there feeling like I had been constipated and was finally able to take a shit! I thought about my money and my ring, and hopped up.

When Chuck came back out of the bathroom, he looked down at my hairy pussy and licked his lips. He pushed me back on the couch with one hand and laid my three thousand dollars next to me. Chuck spread my pussy lips open and flicked his tongue lightly on my clit.

"Shit … my … ring. Oh … oh … my … ring … Chuck!"

I could feel myself cumming. I tried to slide away, but there was nowhere to go. My pussy muscles tightened up, and cum spilled out of me. I lay there moaning as Chuck stood up and aimed his six-inch dick at my pussy hole. He slipped right in and fucked me as hard as he could. I yelled my ass off. Not because he was doing anything to my pussy, but because I was about to get that seven thousand dollar ring that I had seen.

"Get it baby ... it's yours ... get it!"

I reached down and opened my pussy lips so he could see his white dick disappearing into my pussy. Damn, I felt myself cumming again.

"Oh ... Oh ... Oh!" I moaned.

Chuck released his nut in my pussy. I didn't care. He was filthy rich. His daddy had left him millions of dollars and the jewelry store. Shit, he can give me a baby; I know we'll be straight.

After we washed up, Chuck led me to the jewelry case so I could get my ring. I kissed Chuck on the lips, which still smelled like my pussy. I wondered if his wife be smelling that.

I walked out of the jewelry store ten thousand dollars richer. Now, y'all bitches tell me what black men coming off money like that for a virgin asshole and some pussy. Y'all bitches better get it together!

2 Months Later

I can't believe I haven't seen my period in two months. I feel like shit. I don't know about any of y'all, but my pussy keep soaking my panties, and I can't stop throwing up. My mother had got off work early and caught me bent over the toilet, butt naked, throwing up. Brown skinned, 5'7", 150 pounds with hazel brown eyes and jet black hair that hung down her back, she could pass for my damn sister.

"Bitch, if you're pregnant, you're getting out of my damn house!" she screamed.

"Ain't nobody pregnant, Ma!"

"You better hope not!"

"Ma, I got money, I don't have to live here. I stay here just to help you with the bills."

"I paid these bills by myself before you were born."

I just knew that I was pregnant. I picked up the phone and called Chuck.

"White Diamonds, Chuck speaking."

"I'm pregnant!" I blurted out.

"You're what!"

"You heard me, Chuck, don't play!"

"Come by the store so we can talk."

In my 1985 white Cutlass Supreme, I thought about how pretty my baby would be the whole ride to the jewelry store. I pulled in front of the store and got out.

Chuck opened the door in a hurry, pulled me inside, and put the closed sign up.

"I thought you were on the pill," Chuck said with anger.

"Did I ever tell you that?"

"Well, no, but this is what I'm gonna do. I'm gonna give you fifty thousand dollars to have an abortion and forget about me."

This motherfucker done lost his mind if he think I'm gonna get rid of my baby! I'm going to take his money, though. He didn't give me a chance to say yes or no anyway. He wrote me a check, handed it to me, and pushed me out of the door without saying another word.

I walked to my car and headed straight to deposit my money in the bank.

I hid my pregnancy as best I could, but after three more months had gone by, I wasn't able to hide it from my mother. She did as she said and kicked my ass out. I rented a one bedroom apartment in a mostly white neighborhood. I met this white girl who stayed two apartments down named Sarra. She was about twenty years old, with blond hair and blue eyes.

Sarra came by the house on the regular. We were two opposites. She'd never had a white dick, and I'd never had a black dick. One night, Sarra was at my house and we were bored out of our minds. I watched Sarra smoke a joint and wondered how it tasted and made her feel.

"Let me hit that," I said.

Sarra didn't think twice and handed me the joint. She didn't even seem high.

I took two hard pulls and started coughing. I was high as hell; even my baby seemed to have relaxed as I continued to smoke.

Sarra got up and used the phone.

"I'm over my friend's house," she said into the phone.

"Who is that?" I asked.

"My friend, Johnny," Sarra said. "No, she don't like black guys … Yes, she's black."

"Don't say that, damn," I said and laughed.

"You don't." Sarra laughed along with me. "He said can him and his boy come over here and chill?"

"I don't care."

About twenty minutes later, Johnny and his friend, Man, showed up at my house. Johnny was medium height with a slim build, brown skinned, a tiny afro, and a full beard. Man was short, light skinned, with freckles. Johnny and man both wore white button up shirts, blue jeans, and dirty buck shoes. They brought a case of beer and more weed. Next thing I know, we had a full party going.

Johnny pulled out some cocaine and Sarra hopped in his lap like she was riding his dick. They fed each other tokes of the powder. I soon found myself reaching for the coke and taking two tokes myself.

My head fell back on the couch, high out of my mind. I remember Sarra asking me something, then guiding Johnny to the back room.

Man sat in the chair, snapping his finger to the Temptations. The moans coming from the room damn near drowned out the music. I had to pee. I walked past my room and saw Johnny pulling his dick out of Sarra. I don't care if y'all believe me or not, but that nigga's dick looked like two summer sausages. I watched him pull Sarra's white cheeks apart and push half of it in her pussy. She trembled all over as she came.

I thought I was cumming until I felt between my legs and realized I had pissed on myself. I rushed to the bathroom and took a quick shower. Before I could get out, Johnny walked in the bathroom. The nigga was naked. I watched him pull the skin back on his uncircumcised dick and pee. I could see Sarra lying on my bed like she was asleep. After I had dried off, I stepped out of the shower and tried to wrap the towel around my naked body.

Johnny snatched my towel, but I was so high and my mouth felt so numb, I didn't even try to stop him as he spun me around. To keep from falling, I grabbed the top of the toilet bar. Johnny rubbed his dick head between my pussy lips. I felt my nut build just by him doing that. He kept doing it. I rocked back and forth on the head of his dick and soon coated it with thick white cum. It had been so long since I had been fucked. Me being so high, I forgot this nigga had an elephant trunk. He pushed in my pussy. I let out a scream, and he only had the head in. By the time he got four inches in, I had cum twice.

"Damn!" Johnny said, gritting his teeth and moving in and out.

He kept saying damn over and over. I moved my ass in circles on his dick. Johnny pushed two more inches in and cum dripped out of my pussy onto the floor. He sped up fucking me. Johnny had my pussy stretched to the max. I screamed my ass off until he pulled out.

When I looked back, he had walked out of the bathroom. I washed between my legs, put my robe on, and went into the front room. Sarra was riding Johnny's dick on the couch while Man fucked her in the ass. She sucked on two of her fingers to keep from screaming. Man's dick was at least ten inches and thick. This bitch could take some dick!

Man saw me looking, so he pulled out of Sarra's ass and walked past me to the bathroom. I got the powder off the table and started sniffing. Man called my name and I got up and went to the back room. He was lying on my bed stroking his dick. I don't even remember taking my robe off. All I remember is trying to lift up off of his dick after I felt it in my stomach. Man pulled me back down. I moved up and down on his dick slowly until I felt myself cumming. Then I sped up.

"Oh … oh … oh … oh!" I moaned as cum ran down his dick.

He grabbed my waist and continued to move me up and down. He reached back and spread my cheeks as I rode his dick. I felt somebody climb onto the bed, then a tongue slide in my asshole. Tears gathered in my eyes. I came so hard that I think I fainted. All I remember is waking up with a swollen pussy, and Sarra's pussy by my face.

"Bitch, get your pussy out of my face!" I screamed.

Sarra woke up, slid down, and laid her head on my chest. I pushed her off of me and she jumped up.

"What's your problem?" Sarra yelled.

"I don't do the gay shit!"

"You sucked all the cum out of my pussy last night, so bitch don't even go there!"

"Just get the fuck out!" I said, feeling my baby kick.

Two more months went by, and I found myself with an addiction. Cocaine had me gone. Most of my money was gone, and I was getting fucked by a different dick every night. I had caught gonorrhea twice. The worst part about it was, I couldn't get high off of coke anymore. One of the white guys that I was fucking had showed me how to use baking soda to make crack. One night, I decided that I wanted to get super high. I put a twenty cent piece on my stem, put it to my lips, and took a deep hit. I tried to hold it in until I felt like my lungs would collapse.

The sensation of something running down my leg startled me. I blew the smoke out and looked down. It was a clear type of liquid. I put my robe on and ran to Sarra's house. She opened the door with a big black man standing behind her. I passed out right in front of her door.

That night, I gave birth to a premature baby girl. She was four pounds and one ounce. I was so high when I had her, that I don't remember pushing her out. I named her Arkeba Kenyatta Towns. She was a mix of me and her father. When I got enough strength, I limped to the bathroom, grabbing my pocketbook on the way there. I had to celebrate my baby. I pulled my stem out and hit me a nice piece of rock. Shit, I brought a baby into this fucked up world. Don't y'all bitches even hate, she's prettier than y'all baby!

I was released while Arkeba got better. I had to go tell Chuck about our baby. I walked into the jewelry store and Chuck was leaned over the glass counter talking to a mixed girl that I had gone to school with. I walked up, hair all over the place, and stepped between them. The girl walked off with her nose turned up.

"Our baby is beautiful, Chuck!" I said with excitement.

"We don't have a baby, now leave before I call the police!" he said angrily.

"You know what, Chuck? Fuck you, I'll see your ass in court!"

Chuck reached out and grabbed me by my fucking throat! I could feel the air leaving my body. The only thing that I could do was reach in my bra and pull out my stem. I put it to his eye and pushed. He dropped me to the floor and grabbed his eye.

I crawled out of the jewelry store, trying to catch my breath. Once I reached the pavement, I got up, ran to my car, and took off. I pulled up in front of my apartment and ran inside. I had a dime piece of crack in my drawer. My stem still had Chuck's blood up there, but I didn't care. I needed this hit to get my mind right. My mind always became worry free after my hit.

Johnny and Man had moved up and were now the men to see for almost every drug known to man. They couldn't get enough of my pussy, so I called Man to get some credit until I go to the bank. I needed another hit bad.

Ten minutes later, Man got out of Johnny's shiny black Corvette in a white Brooks Brothers suit and gray gators. Johnny must be driving Man's white Camaro.

"What's up, Case?" Man asked, walking through the door.

"I need a fifty cent piece until I go to the bank tomorrow."

"I need something now to make sure that you will pay me."

"I don't have anything. You know I'm good for it."

"You have something I have wanted for so long."

"I just had a baby, Man. I'm bleeding."

"Not out of your ass."

"You're too big!" I whined.

"Alright, call me when you get the money." He started walking toward the door.

I slid my pants down so my pad wouldn't fall out, and only the back of my ass showed. Man turned me around and dropped his pants.

"Don't cry, Case. You'll like it once I get it in, I promise."

Man went in his pants and handed me two fifty cent (dollar) pieces of crack. My tears went away fast. He was so gentle. Man kissed and sucked on my ass cheeks, leaving passion marks. I moaned with pleasure. It seemed like the more I moaned, the more blood ran out of my pussy into my pad. I heard Man spitting on something. I couldn't look back at his dick, I probably would've fainted.

As Man was easing his dick head in my ass, I put a nice piece on my stem, put it to my lips and lit my lighter. I pulled on my stem as he pushed in. It felt like a telephone pole was being pushed up my ass. The crack hit my lungs and my body went numb. Man moved in and out of me, but I almost felt nothing. I blew out the smoke and my body regained its feeling. Man slid more dick into my ass, and I tried to crawl away, but he held my hips and kept pumping.

"That's enough, Man!" I screamed, "Oh ... Man ... oh ...!"

Man didn't stop until he came in my ass. When he pulled out, shit shot all over his dick and pants. Seeing the evil look in his eyes, I tried to run, but my pants were still down, causing me to fall. Instead of Man beating me, he grabbed me by my hair, snatched my pants down, and ran his shitty dick all the way in my pussy, knocking my stitches loose. I scratched and clawed his back and the floor until I passed out.

I woke up in a puddle of blood, with a bloody, shitty rag on my face. For the second time that day, I crawled across the floor, this time to the bathroom and ran me a tub of water. After sliding into the water, I thought about how I could get money out of Chuck. I soaked until the water turned warm then got out of the tub, limped to the phone, and called Chuck at the store.

"White Diamonds, Chuck speaking!"

"Listen, Chuck, all I'm asking for is ten thousand up front and two thousand a month child support."

"Listen, you nigger bitch, you and that nigger baby won't get a dime of my money!"

"Alright, I'll see you in court. I wonder how your wife will react to this."

"Okay ... okay ... where do I send the money?" Chuck asked, defeated.

"For the pain and suffering of you calling me and your child a nigger, I want you to make it fifty thousand up front and thirty-five hundred a month!" I smiled, knowing that I had him in the palm of my hand. "Send it to my bank account by 3:00 today!" I said and hung up.

I went to the bank at 3:40 to see if the money had been deposited, and it was there. I withdrew $1,000 and called Man. He answered the phone with church music playing in the background. Man was really crazy.

"I got your money for the stuff," I said.

"Oh, we good. Girl, that ass of yours is out of this world."

I hung up on his ass. As I thought about how he put that big ass dick in me, I started smoking, and before I knew it, a whole week had gone by. I hadn't been to check on my baby, so I got up, put some clothes on and went to the hospital.

When I walked into the room, my mother was sitting in a chair with Arkeba in her arms. She stopped humming softly when she looked up and saw me. Ma hopped up and put her hand over her mouth. I know I looked bad, but damn she didn't have to do all of that. She put Arkeba in her car seat, walked up to me, and slapped blood out of my mouth.

"Bitch, I don't know what has got into you, but you're gonna take care of this baby!" Ma said through gritted teeth. "Sign these papers so I can take my grandbaby home!" She pushed the papers to my damn chest.

"Don't hit me no damn more!" I said, getting loud.

I saw that she wasn't backing down, and mama used to brawl with the best of them. I signed the birth certificate and put Chuck's name down as the father. My mother snatched the papers and took them to the nurse. I watched my baby lay there watching me, as tears rolled down my face. I leaned over and kissed her cheeks and watched them turn red. I thought about how I had slapped Chuck's ass, and his face and ass had turned red.

I went shopping for my baby and took her home to our one bedroom apartment. Her crib was right beside my bed. As I got her settled, I heard a knock at the door. I rushed to the door, and my mother stood there with two plates of food in her hand. I let her in and went to the back where my baby was. I heard my mother in the front room cleaning up, so I went to help her.

Someone knocked at the door again, and Johnny and Man walked in with two bags of clothes, bears, balloons, and a case of beer.

My mother looked at them, got her purse and walked out without saying a word.

It took less than three months for me to go through the fifty thousand dollars, and Chuck had stopped depositing my money. Arkeba seemed to shit out diapers more and more every day. I called the shop over and over, and Chuck's wife said he wasn't there. Finally fed up with him avoiding me, I got Arkeba dressed and went to the jewelry store. Keba and I walked in, and Chuck was showing an old white lady a platinum bracelet. He lost all train of thought when he saw me with Arkeba.

The white lady gave him her credit card and Chuck rushed off. He brought the lady her receipt and escorted her to the door. Once she was gone, he flipped the sign over and walked toward me with his fist balled up.

"Didn't I tell you …" Chuck said, cutting himself off after he looked down and saw Arkeba staring at him.

He walked over to her car seat and rubbed the side of her face. Arkeba blew out spit bubbles. Chuck stood up, walked to the back and brought me back five thousand dollars. He kissed my forehead and walked away. I walked out of the store and got into my car to go get me some crack. Y'all bitches still hating on me. Yeah, I'm a crack head with a pretty baby and a rich baby daddy. I told y'all bitches from the beginning about that rich white dick.

Chapter 2

Arkeba Towns

16 years later ...

My mama wasn't paying the bills, so we had to move back with my grandmama. She made me promise that I wouldn't tell Grandma the nasty, freaky stuff I've seen her do, but it stayed in my head. I'm happy to be here with Grandma because she spoils me. My mama is never around anyway. I hope she shows up for my birthday party tomorrow.

I have someone to tell all of my deepest secrets. My friend, Jason. He's the same age I am, black as night, about 5'7, 135 pounds. He got kind of big eyes, and always wear a ponytail on top of his head. He lives next door to us. We have seen our mothers do a lot of stuff, and we both have been through a lot. I think we keep each other happy.

"Don't stand there watching me, looking like a skinny ass Michael Jackson with a ponytail!" I heard Grandma say. "Take your ass back there where Keba at."

Grandma had been in the front room writing her numbers,

so I know Jason must have come in. She talks so bad to him. I sat on the bed and listened to my mama's Keith Sweat CD. Keith Sweat sang "Make It Last Forever," like no other. Jason pushed my door open, came into the room, and closed it. I lay on my bed in a mini skirt. Jason lip-synced along with Keith Sweat, rubbing his flat chest like he had breasts. Grandma opened the door and caught him.

"Boy, you better sit your little sissy ass down! I'm going to put my numbers in, I'll be back," she said and closed my room door.

I laughed so hard at Grandma catching Jason, I had to pee. Jason started tickling me, making me wet my panties a little. I pushed him away and ran to the bathroom. After peeing, I went back into my room and found Jason trying on one of my tank tops with the pink bow at the top. I threw my wet panties at him.

"See what you made me do."

Jason picked my panties up and smelled the seat.

"Eww, Jason, you are nasty!" I said, laughing at him.

"Wait, so that mean you're naked under that?" Jason asked, pointing at my skirt.

Being around my mama all of them years, I didn't have a choice but to be hot in the ass. I lifted up my skirt and showed Jason. We both laughed as I sat on the bed. Jason came close to me, squatted down and looked between my legs.

"What are you doing?" I asked.

"I want to see what it look like up close."

I didn't really think anything of it. I pulled my skirt up and showed Jason my cake.

"I saw my mama's friend lick her down there, and she kept calling his name," Jason said.

Jason licked me on my cake lips. I called his name over and over while laughing.

"No, wait, he did this," Jason said then opened my cake and licked between my slit.

I stopped laughing and took a deep breath. It was a feeling that

I never felt. He kept doing it. I found my little young fifteen-year-old ass lying on the bed, moaning Jason's name. We were so into it that we didn't hear Grandma open my door.

"Get y'all grown asses up!" Grandma yelled.

She rushed off and came back with a leather belt. Grandma had never beaten me, but when I saw her grab Jason and begin putting hand licks against his legs, ass, and back, I knew that I was next! Jason screamed for his mama. Grandma let him go and grabbed me.

"You … gonna … be just … like…your … sorry … ass… mama!" she screamed with every swing.

She beat my ass like a runaway slave. When Grandma got through with me, I had welts all over my yellow body. Through all of that ass whipping, I still couldn't believe how good getting licked down there felt.

The next day, I had my birthday party. My mama showed up smelling like fish, but I love her and was happy that she was there. Grandma told her what Jason and I had done. She yelled at me to come here. I thought she was going to tear my ass up. When I got close, she pulled me to her.

"Don't be letting any man touch you unless he pays for it. You're too pretty not to get paid," Ma whispered in my ear. I shook my head up and down. My mama winked at me and said out loud, "I'll kill your ass if I hear it again!"

I was so embarrassed, but most of the kids there had mothers who smoked crack too. Jason stopped playing and looked at me. He blew a kiss at me, making me smile at his crazy self. I was back to normal. Jason always knew what to do to make me feel better.

A delivery truck pulled up. A white man got out with a package. Every one of my birthdays, I got delivered a package. After my grandmamma signed for it, she handed it to me. I opened it with a big smile. It was a locket with a key to it, a diary, and a check for twenty thousand dollars. Grandma fanned herself with the check and told me to go play. I ran where my friends were so I could show them what I got. Jason was chasing them around the house with a muddy dildo that he had found in his backyard. They screamed and ran from him until Grandma saw what he had.

"Bring your ass here, Boy George!" Grandma yelled.

Jason tried to sling the dildo. He drew back like a girl. The dildo slipped out of his hand and hit Grandma in the face, knocking her reading glasses off. Jason stood there stuck. He started crying, and then ran home. A lot of kids's already called him gay. Now they were gonna start calling him cry baby. Grandma picked up her glasses and the muddy dildo. She walked into the house and slammed the door. My mother went in behind her, begging for money.

After the party, I snuck over to Jason's house to check on him. I always walk straight into his house. Jason's mother was walking from the back room naked. She is about 36 years old, jet black, 5'9", and 180 pounds, with long dreads. She's full-blooded Jamaican. We call her Jean.

"What I tell your half white ass about just walking up in here?" Jean said in her Jamaican accent as she lit a cigarette.

"He's back there in his room. You and him need to go somewhere and play because I have company on the way."

I walked down the hallway to Jason's room. His room was a mess! He had only a mattress that sat on the floor as his bed, and his clothes were in a black plastic trash bag like he was visiting. He had a small TV that sat on cement blocks, with a sheet over the blocks.

"Tell your mama to put some clothes on. She got all of that hair down there," I said, pointing at my cake.

"Can you keep a secret?" Jason asked, putting his game on pause.

"You know that I can."

Jason got up, went up under his mattress, and pulled out a chrome gun.

"It's a nine millimeter!" Jason said with excitement.

"Boy, where did you get that from?" I whispered.

"My mama had this man over here last night. He left his keys on the table, I took them and searched his car. I found it under his seat."

"What are you gonna do with it?"

"I'm gonna be a hitman. People gonna pay me to kill people!"

"You are crazy, Jason."

"Keba, I'm not gay either, I like girls."

"You like me, Jason?" I asked, turning around and dancing.

He blushed.

I heard my grandma yelling my name, so I ran out of Jason's room. His mother lay on her bed, sucking a man's dick with the door cracked. That was my first time seeing a dick that close.

My grandmother watched me run out of Jason's house. I looked back and saw Jason looking out of his window at me. I blew him a kiss.

"You better stay away from over there, all them men that be in and out of that house. Don't come running home saying your fast ass got raped," Grandma said.

I went to my room to prepare for school. I put out an outfit I got for my birthday. My grandma was supposed to give me fifteen hundred dollars to go shopping. I wanted to buy Jason some stuff because I didn't want people to keep picking at him. His crazy ass already has a gun.

The next day, Jason and I were on our way home from school. Guys always called my name, stared at my ass, or my tiny breasts. A black Benz pulled up beside us. The tinted window came down, and a light skinned guy in a suit sat there looking at me. He looked just like a light skinned Chris Tucker.

"Come here, girl!" he said.

Jason followed me to the car.

"Nigga, I didn't call your ugly ass!"

"Where she goes, I go, nigga!" Jason said, grilling the man and pulling me away from the car.

We kept walking. The man rode slowly beside us.

"I just wanted to ask y'all do y'all want a job. The pay is real good."

Jason and I stopped walking. Jason walked to the car. I followed behind him.

"What we got to do? Really, I'm a hit man," Jason said.

The man burst out laughing.

"What's so damn funny?" Jason asked with attitude.

"Your little ass ain't killing nothing."

"I'll kill you if a motherfucker pays me enough."

The guy stopped laughing when he saw that Jason was serious.

"I tell you what, killer, if you're about that, be at my house at 3:30 tomorrow. Here's some money for cab fare." He wrote his address on a fifty dollar bill, balled it up, and threw it out the window.

Jason picked the money up and we watched him drive away. We talked about it all the way home.

"Alright, my love, see you tomorrow."

My grandma was sound asleep when I walked into the house. She lay on the couch snoring. I walked past her to my room. Jason's skinny pit bull kept barking. I looked out my window to see what he was barking at. Jason stood in front of his dog with that gun pointed at the dog's head. He smiled at the dog, then pulled the trigger. The dog fell over and Jason ran back into the house.

Grandma rolled off the couch onto the floor. I ran in the front room and saw her on the floor with her head covered. She talks all that shit, but she scary as hell.

"What the fuck was that?" Grandma asked, getting up off of the floor.

"It was a raggedy car driving by."

After doing my homework, I called my friend girls and told them lies about Jason and I having sex, and how he was not gay. They didn't believe me because they weren't having sex yet. I lay down. My mind went to thinking about tomorrow, and about Jason killing that dog with a smile on his face.

I met Jason in front of his house. Jason came out in the same pants that he had worn the day before, a wrinkled white tee, and white Air Ones that had seen better days. He is my closest friend, though. Jason is the only one to have seen me naked, and the only one who has put his hands on me. I know that I'm only sixteen years old, but I want him to do it again.

"Jason, why do you like girl clothes?" I asked.

"Really, I prefer boy clothes, but you're my only friend, and your grandma keeps your clothes so clean and white. They feel good against my skin, so I figure only girl clothes feel like that."

"That's not true, boys' clothes feel the same way. I'll buy you some clothes today, and when you need them washed, I'll wash them for you, okay?"

"You don't have to do —"

"I want to, you're my friend," I said, cutting him off and rubbing his dusty ponytail.

My friends met Jason and me at the corner of the school. They didn't understand why I hung with Jason. Hands down, I was one of the prettiest, if not the prettiest girl at the school. All the boys tried their best to get me. I pulled Jason along with the girls. They know Jason and I stayed together like glue.

Before Jason went to his class, I pulled him to me and kissed him on his lips. All the girls made a nasty face, and all the guys grilled Jason. I didn't care; I just wanted things to feel normal for him. Jason walked away smiling, showing those pretty white teeth.

Through the whole school day, I kept thinking about why Jason told that man he was a hit man. I seemed to have daydreamed the whole day away. Before I knew it, school was letting out. I met Jason in front of his locker. He seemed calm about what we were going to do.

"Are we still catching a cab to that man's house?" I asked.

"No, I changed my mind. Let's go home," Jason said.

Jason and I began to walk home. The same black Benz pulled up beside us. The tinted window rolled down slowly, and the man stuck his head out the window.

"I knew y'all were bullshitting," he said. Laughing, he opened the passenger door. "Come on and get in, little lady, I need to talk to you."

I don't know what came over me; I went and got into his car. Jason stood there looking at me.

"Come on, Jason," I said.

"No, I got a bad feeling about this."

"Just come on, we won't be long."

Jason walked slowly to the car. He threw his dirty jean backpack in the back seat and got in. Jason watched the jewelry on the man's hand and neck, and his high-priced clothes.

"My name is Frank, and I'm kind of new in this area. I'm originally from Detroit. I just started this new business, and I'm looking for some young guys like yourself to help me out. The pay is good, and y'all don't have to be hit men." He laughed.

"What do we have to do?" I asked.

"I'll talk to y'all about that when we get to my crib. Are y'all down?"

I looked back at Jason and smiled, then said, "Yes."

Frank pulled off, if that's his real name. He drove until we pulled up in front of a baby mansion in Rocky Mount. His house was huge. He had to have some money. I might as well enjoy, cause Grandma gonna fuck me up for coming home late. We walked in the house and I just stood there for a moment, looking around at all the nice furniture.

"I don't have much time, so follow me and I'll show y'all what to do."

"We gotta hurry and get home," Jason said.

Frank looked at Jason and frowned.

"Maybe I should just show y'all," Frank said, going to his DVD player.

He inserted a DVD. Moans came through the surround sound, and then a girl and a guy about Jason and my age were on a bed doing the nasty. I started laughing until I saw blood on the sheets.

Apple Tree

"Why are you showing us this?" I asked.

"I wanted to pay you to have sex with one of my little homies your age, but since you brought the sissy boy, I'll pay you both to do each other."

"We're not doing that!" Jason said. "Take us home!"

"I'll pay y'all five hundred dollars each," Frank said.

Jason put his book bag on his back and walked toward the door. I stood there thinking about what my mama had said, *Don't let any man touch you for free.*

"Wait, Jason, let me talk to you," I said, pulling him with me a distance away from Frank. "Look, we can use the money. You need new clothes, and I had seen this bracelet in the mall in Raleigh that I want."

Jason stood there thinking for a minute. I wanted to do it anyway, so why not get paid like mama told me?

"I'll do it because you want me to," Jason said, "but I still don't think this is a good idea. Let's see if we can get more money out of him." Jason looked at Frank. "Alright, we'll do it, but you have to pay us one thousand a piece up front." Jason stuck out his hand.

Frank went to a picture on his wall and pulled it out. A safe was behind it. Jason and I watched as he turned the combination. He opened the safe, pulled out two small stacks and handed them to Jason. He took them both and stuffed them in his pocket.

"Alright, follow me," Frank said and smiled. "What I am doing is illegal, so we have to keep this between us."

As we followed Frank, I began to tremble badly. I thought about the blood that came from that girl. I had just gone off of my period last week; I thought it was her time of the month. We walked down to the basement. A big black guy stood over one of the lights adjusting it so it would shine on the bed. He was tall and at least three hundred pounds of all muscle, even in his damn head. He scared me even more.

"We don't have to do it in front of y'all, do we?" I asked.

"No, we'll be in the next room looking at the monitors," Frank said.

Jason stood there quiet.

"Alright, y'all get undressed. I'll tell y'all what to do as y'all go along," Frank said.

"No, we will just do it!" Jason said.

"Whatever, let's get started."

Frank and the big guy walked out of the room. I began taking off my clothes. I was scared, but at the same time, it felt right. Jason turned his back to me and took his clothes off. I heard Frank and the big guy laughing.

"Damn, punk boy, you got something nice down there," Frank said.

I still didn't understand what they were talking about until Jason turned around. Jason's dick was about seven and a half inches soft, and big around like a pickle. I had a change of heart right then. Jason moved his lips, saying that we could fake it. I was with that. I lay back on the bed.

Jason had watched his mother and her lovers so much, that he knew everything to do. He climbed on top of me and tongue kissed me. Jason went down to my breast and put my nipple in his mouth. The feeling was unreal, then he went to my other one. I begin to move under him, I couldn't be still. He moved down to my cake and licked me like he did the last time. I started seeing stars, and my ears started popping. Damn, this was worth all the money in the world! I felt like I had to pee, my whole body trembled. I felt. I felt … I felt … Jason stopped.

I opened my eyes and shook my head, like 'why did you stop?' His dick was sticking straight out. He laid it on my stomach and faked like he was inside me humping. I didn't know that I was supposed to moan or yell. Frank burst into the room with a machete in his hand.

"Do y'all think I'm stupid?" he said. "Either you put that dick in her, or I'll chop it off, punk boy!"

I was scared as fuck! I whispered for Jason to do it. What the fuck did I tell him that for? He aimed at my cake entrance and pushed. I let out a loud scream. Jason tried to stop, but I didn't want the man to cut us up. I pulled him in further. Something broke loose, and the rest slid in. I felt something running out of me and knew that it was blood. Once Jason was all the way in, he just stayed there.

"Move in and out, punk boy!" Frank said. "Zoom in on this!" he told the big guy.

Jason moved in and out. It hurt so damn bad. It felt like he was pulling something out of me! The pain began to go away, and I started moaning and moving my hips. I could not keep still. Jason stared me in my eyes as he moved in and out, then he closed them and I felt something warm shoot in me. Jason fell on top of me, breathing hard. When he slid out of my cake, it felt like he was still in there. I was hurting again, and it ached.

"Now do it again," Frank said.

"No, I'm hurting!" I said.

"Either y'all do it again, or I will kill you both!" Frank yelled.

"She said she was hurting, take us the fuck home!" Jason said, grilling Frank.

The big guy came into the room.

"Put your clothes on," Frank said.

After Jason put his clothes on, the big guy pulled him by his arm out of the room. Jason reached down and grabbed his backpack. Once the door was closed, Frank started taking his clothes off.

"You, little girl, got the body of a goddess," he said as I backed up into a corner, still feeling blood run in my panties.

Frank grabbed me and threw me back on the bed. My face landed on the blood that had come out of me. I screamed for dear life! Frank climbed on top of me and ripped my panties off. I yelled Jason's name over and over. All of a sudden, I heard a gunshot, then another. Frank jumped up, ran up the basement stairs, and out the door.

Jason

There ain't no damn way I'm going out like that! Y'all are not gonna believe what this big muscle bound motherfucker did! He pulled me out of the room. Soon as the door closed, he pushed me to the floor, dropped his pants, and told me to suck his dick! He had the nerve to fart and start picking his teeth with a toothpick. I got on my knees, unzipped my backpack, grabbed my gun, and aimed at his dick. I pulled the trigger and watched his dick and balls blow the fuck off! He fell over, trying to catch his breath. His lips moved, but no words came out. I squatted down in front of him, aimed my gun at his mouth, and blew his teeth and tongue out the back of his head. What a feeling! It almost felt better than busting my first nut. I sat there staring at the body for a minute. Now let me go save Keba.

Frank burst through the door in all of his jewelry, butt naked, except some black dress socks. His eyes went straight to the big guy's body with blood pouring out the back of his head. He turned and looked at me. I had the gun aimed at his dick.

"Hold, hold it, I got money, chill," Frank stuttered.

"Arkeba, are you all right?" I yelled.

Keba came out of the basement with her torn panties in her hand. She ran and wrapped her arms around me until she saw the body lying on the floor. She fell to her knees crying and then threw up.

"I promise I won't call the cops!" Frank said with his hands in the air.

"Open that safe, and get up, Keba!" I said, aiming the gun at Frank. The gun began to feel heavy in my small arms. Frank moved too fast.

"Stop nigga!" Frank stopped in his tracks. "Keba, get up and open the safe." Arkeba got up and pushed a chair to the wall, so she could reach the picture. "Tell her the code or I'll blow your dick off!"

"Alright ... chill little man. 25 ... 22 ... 21 ... right ... 22 ... 18 ... left," Frank said.

Keba turned the knob as he talked. The safe came open. She looked back at me. Her tears had turned into a smile.

"There's a lot of money in here!" she said with excitement.

"Get something to put it in!" I said.

Keba ran to the basement and came back with two pillowcases. She filled the cases up with money. Keba pulled out three packages with black tar stamped on them and two guns. We didn't know what that black tar shit was. I started to tell her to put it back, but I thought about the movie, *Menace II Society*, and how O-dog shot the Chinese man in the store and got the tape.

"Give me the disk of us, nigga!" I said, pointing the gun.

"It's in the back, just be easy with that gun!" Frank said.

"Go get the disk, Keba!"

Keba ran to the back and soon returned with the disk.

"Take the stuff to the car!" I instructed Keba.

"Come on, Jason, we gotta go!" she began to cry again.

"I'm right behind you."

Keba pulled the pillow cases with her out of the door.

"Let me get that chain and them rings too, nigga!" I said, aiming the gun at his chest.

Frank acted like he was going to take his chain off, but ran toward me instead. I hit the trigger twice, stopping his bitch ass in his tracks. Frank grabbed his wounded chest, as blood poured out. He caught the blood with his hands and tried to push it back into his chest. Frank tried to talk, but blood dripped out the corner of his mouth. He took another step toward me, and I shot his ass two more times. He dropped to the floor dead. I went over to him, slid his chains and rings off, as he shitted on himself.

I ran out of the house, jumped in Frank's Benz with Keba, and she took off out of the driveway.

"Slow down, you're gonna get us pulled over!" I said, tightening the rubber band around my ponytail.

"I don't know which way to go!" Keba cried.

"Stop that crying!" I said. "We gotta be strong. We can't tell anyone about this. Keep going until you see a sign."

Keba and I rode around until we saw a sign that said, Tarboro exit next right. I was so relieved. We rode back to Tarboro in silence. It was dark when we finally made it back to our neighborhood. Keba got out down the street from the house, and I took off. I backed the car up in my yard, ran and took the cases in the house, then I ran back to the car and took off. I drove the car to the other side of town, wiped the inside and outside door handles down, and left the car on the side of the road. I had run about four blocks before I slowed down. My gun was getting heavier and heavier. Running track in school had paid off. I stopped at an Arab store breathing hard.

The Arab watched every step I took in his store. I bought a juice and a chicken sandwich then walked out of the store. I went to the pay phone, called a cab to the address across the street from the store, and hid on the side of the house until the cab pulled up. I ran and hopped into the cab like I lived there.

Leaning back in the cab, I wiped the sweat off of my face. I smelled Keba's pussy on my hands. I had to smile. Now I got bragging rights. I finally got me some from the prettiest girl at the school. The cab dropped me off at the store down from my house. I ran all the way home and tip-toed to my room. Soon as I closed my room door, I saw a car pull into the driveway. I was scared almost to fucking death! I ran to the front of the house and looked out the window. My mama got out of the car and came into the house. A man walked in behind her.

"Where in the fuck have you been, Jay?" she yelled in her Jamaican accent. "You had me worried sick!"

"I was at my friend's house playing, Ma!" I said in my little boy voice.

The man looked at me and smiled. He wore a Rocawear tee shirt, gray Rocawear jeans, an all-white Rocawear fitted, and all-white ones. I looked out the window. He was driving an old black Corvette. My mama pulled him by his arm to her room and closed the door. I soon heard Ma moaning real loud.

I went to my room and pulled my other two guns out of the pillow case. I had fallen in love with guns that fast.

"So … Big … So… fat!" Mama moaned.

I turned my video game and radio on to block that out. My mama doesn't do drugs. I came to the conclusion that she just loves to get fucked, and plenty of niggas kick out for it. She never worked, and pays all the bills. She goes to cooking school, and to community college studying business. I'm about to hold her down, so she won't have to do all that sex shit. I'm the man of this house. I never met my pops. My mama says she doesn't know who he is, so I just let it go. I lay down, and looked at my two guns, shining from the light. I smoked them bitch ass niggas.

I hopped up. I gotta go check on Keba.

Annette Towns: BKA Grandma Towns or Towns

This little hoe done lost her damn mind! She doesn't come straight home from school, then she got the nerve to come home smelling like sex. I beat her ass in her back until her panties with blood on them fell out of her little ass bra. I went crazy on her ass then. She is not gonna be like her sorry ass mama!

I was supposed to have a date tonight, but I had to ride around looking for her hot ass. Done ran my damn blood pressure up. I know that bad ass sissy boy had something to do with my baby having sex. Her period just went off, so I know it wasn't that, and her panties were ripped. It's something she's not telling me, but the truth will come out. What goes on in the dark always comes to the light.

I might as well go ahead and tell y'all that dildo that bad ass boy found was mine. I was on my back porch thinking how I let my friend fuck me in the same spot. I had my skirt up, going to work with my toy, about to cum. Arkeba came home from school early, walking through the house yelling my name. I knew that she was on her way to the back porch. I slung my toy in that Jamaican whore's yard. That skinny ass dog ran and grabbed my toy with his mouth, and bit on it like it was bone. I was mad as hell! I wonder what happened to that skinny mutt. I haven't heard him bark lately. I looked out the window and saw that Jamaican whore going in her house. I know that bitch got a wore out pussy! I shut my blind and went to check on my grand baby. I opened her door and she was laid across the bed reading her social studies book. I smiled and closed the door. My baby is an all "A" student. She is gonna become somebody important to the world.

I wonder where her sorry ass mama at. See, I was the same way when I was young. It wasn't nothing for me to hit one of them niggas I fucked with up for some money. I drive a cocaine white 2004 Benz Coupe, and my shit is paid for. Us Towns girls have been known for having that golden pussy since slavery. Shit, we made the slave master leave his damn wife. Do y'all remember that day I left my daughter's house when Johnny and Man walked in? I'm the one that put them niggas on and broke their virginity. Them niggas used to eat out of my damn hands. Yeah, y'all shocked, right? Well, I don't give a fuck because my goddamn pussy gets wet too! I'm going to sleep!

Arkeba

Soon as my grandmamma closed my door, I hopped up and ran to the window. Tears ran down my face. I was so damn scared about what happened today, and I didn't know where Jason had gone. I saw movement at the back of his house and Jason walked out of the dark toward my house. Y'all don't know how happy I was to see him. He crept around to my window, took two cement blocks from the back door steps, and climbed through my window. I jumped in his arms and wrapped my legs around his waist. His skinny body almost fell. I planted my pink lips on his lips, as my tears dropped on his face. It still felt like he was in my cake. I unwrapped my legs from around him and stepped back.

"I'm still scared!" I cried.

"I got you, okay?" he said and lay me on the bed.

Jason climbed on the bed behind me and held me tight until I fell asleep.

I woke up the next morning and Jason was gone. How about he had gone into my closet and picked me out an outfit to wear. He picked me out my black tank top, Gucci skirt, that I begged my grandmama to buy, and my open toe black red bottom heels. He laid my Gucci purse on top of my skirt. After showering, I put my clothes on. I opened my purse to put my lip gloss inside, and it was stuffed with hundred dollar bills. I put my hand over my mouth to keep from screaming.

I met Jason in front of my house. He stood there in a dingy tee shirt, faded blue jogging pants, and some dirty Air Ones. I thought about him putting his penis in me. I felt wetness running in my panties; I hope it wasn't blood again. Jason looked me up and down and smiled. We walked to school together as usual.

Around twelve o'clock, I went to Jason's class and told him to come out. We skipped the rest of the day, called a cab, and went to the mall in Rocky Mount. I didn't really need anything, so I spent all the money in my purse, and the fifteen hundred dollars Grandma gave me on Jason. We went in almost every store. I made him throw that shit he had on in the trash. He had so many clothes that we had to buy a push cart. Jason never told me how much money was in the pillow cases, and I didn't bother to ask. Jason walked out of the mall in a brown Akademiks tank top, blue Akademiks jeans, and fresh butter Workmen Timbs. I stood on my tiptoes, and gave him a kiss. We loaded the cab down.

By the time we got home, it was 3:05. Jason dropped me off

down the street, so Grandma wouldn't see me get out of the cab. The cab dropped Jason off at home. He unloaded all the bags and went in the house.

Grandma watched me walk up through the window. She rushed out of the house toward me and pulled me in her arms.

"Baby, where have you been?" She began to cry. "I'm so sorry … so sorry!" She cried and rocked me.

"Sorry about what, Grandma? What's going on?" I began to cry.

"They found your mother dead this morning!"

"No… no!"

I fainted right there. I heard everything everyone was saying, I just couldn't open my eyes.

I woke up in the hospital the next day with an IV in my arm. Jason was holding my hand. I smiled when I saw him. I began to think about my mama and started to cry.

"Don't cry, I will find out who did it and murder them!" Jason said.

"We don't know where to even start!" I cried.

"I promise you, I'll get whoever did this, but you gotta promise me that you'll finish school and go to college."

"You can't leave me, Jason. Promise me that you'll never leave."

"I can't, Keba. I can't." He teared up.

I was released from the hospital that evening. When we turned into our driveway, a 2004 Royal Blue 745 Beamer was in Grandma's parking spot. Grandma got out of the car cursing. No one was in the BMW, but there was a card under the windshield wiper. Grandma read it and handed it to me. It said,

Arkeba,

I'm sorry about your mother's death. She was a pretty loving person. If I could bring her back, I would. I know that you are sad. I hope this will cheer you up.

I had to read the card one more time. After rereading the card, I opened the car door. The new leather smell hit me in the nose. A key was in the ignition hooked to a key chain, with my name in small crushed diamonds. I already had my learners permit. My grandma had promised to take me to try for my license soon. Can y'all believe she didn't say anything when I hopped in and backed out of the driveway? I drove straight to Jason's house and blew the horn. His mama came to the door in a see through nightgown. An old black Corvette was parked in the driveway. I rolled the window down. Jean saw that it was me, and she extended her arms like she wanted a hug. I put my car in park and went to give her a hug.

"Baby, I'm so sorry about your mother," she said in her Jamaican accent.

"She's in a better place now," I said. "Is Jason here?"

"No, Jason has been gone all day. Why did you buy him so many clothes?"

"That's my baby," I said and walked back to my car.

His mother smiled from ear to ear. I think she thought Jason was gay too. I wondered where he could be. I drove around the block. He was nowhere to be found. I rode around until a Keith Sweat song came on the radio. It reminded me of my mama, and the fun times we had listening to that song. I became sad and depressed, so I drove back home.

When I pulled up in the driveway, my grandma was on the front porch. She saw the look on my face when I got out of my car and ran off the porch to me.

"What's wrong, baby?" she asked.

"I want my mama!" I cried.

"Come on, baby," Grandma said, hugging me.

I sat down beside my grandma on the porch. A detective car pulled in behind me. A cab turned into Jason's driveway. Jason got out of the cab in a white Polo jogging suit with the Polo sign in red, and white and red Air Ones, with his hair cornrowed. I watched his mother come out of their house with a man on her heels. Grandma looked that way and smiled, then turned back to the detectives walking toward us. It was two white detectives. One was about 40 years old, 5'6", 140 pounds, black hair and a thick mustache. The other detective was about 38 years old, 5'8", 180 pounds, black hair, with no facial hair. They both wore cheap looking blue suits.

"Ms. Towns, I'm Detective Smith, and this is my partner, Detective Ham, we are investigating your daughter's murder," the short detective said.

"How was she murdered?"

"We have reason to believe that somebody wanted us to think that she overdosed on heroin, but we had her system checked, and found no trace of heroin in her body. We checked the needle, and it tested positive for battery acid."

I couldn't take any more. I ran over to where Jason was and hugged him. I watched the detectives get in their car and leave.

"Arkeba!" Johnny said.

I looked at him closely. He had muscles everywhere. I couldn't place him though.

"It's me, your godfather, Johnny!" he said.

"Some … body … killed… my mama!" I cried.

Johnny dropped his head and wiped a tear from his eye.

"I'll be back," Johnny said to Jean and walked over to my house. He sat on the porch with Grandma.

Jean went in the house and brought me out some homemade cookies and a cup of lemonade. The crazy part about all of this is my mama just died, and my mind is on getting Jason to sneak over and fuck me tonight. I know y'all are calling me grown. How old were y'all when y'all started having sex? Shit, my mama just died, I need something big or small to ease my hurt. Don't judge me! I'm just trying to deal with things the best way that I know how.

"Where have you been?" I asked Jason.

"I heard that your mama was murdered, so I had been trying to find out who did it."

"Have you found anything or who did it?"

"The day you fainted, I went across town, and this crackhead lady said somebody brought your mama in the drug spot passed out. The man that owns the house kicked everybody out. She says she heard loud screaming, and then about twenty minutes later, the man that brought her there left, and the ambulance and police came five minutes later."

"Who was the man?"

"She said she didn't know, but he used to pick your mother up and party with her back in the day."

My mind started to roam. I tried hard to place the man, but nothing came to me. I flopped down on the steps and began to cry. Jason sat down beside me. Where did he get that cologne from? It made my cake feel funny. He touched my back and a chill ran all the way down my spine, to my cake. I don't know what the fuck was happening to me. My mind stayed on sex. I pulled out of Jason's reach. He probably thought I didn't want to be touched, but I didn't want to tell him my panties were soaking wet at a time like this. I've never felt like this.

We watched Johnny walk back over to the house. He had a sad look on his face.

"Do you know who used to chill with my mama back in the day?" I asked.

"Honestly, your mama was a wild girl. She chilled with a lot of men."

"Where have you been? I haven't seen you around."

"The feds had me for fifteen and a half long years."

"What did you go for?"

"You're nosey just like your mama," he said. "I went for drugs."

My eyes went from his face to his dick print. What was I thinking? He looked at me and shook his head. I was so embarrassed, but his print was so fucking huge. I found myself daydreaming about begging him to stop.

Jason stood up and took me away from my thoughts.

"Come on," Jason said, going into the house.

I followed him to his room and closed the door.

"Lock the door," he told me.

I locked the door and watched Jason go to the back of his closet and pull the pillow case out. He poured the money on the bed beside the .357 that he had taken out of one of the cases.

"Help me count this shit," Jason said.

"Can we do something first?" I asked shyly.

"Do what?"

"What we did at Frank's house."

Jason smiled at me. "You hooked now, ain't you?"

"No, I know that we will always be friends, but I can't stop thinking about getting fucked by different guys. I love you and always will be loyal to you, but I think I want different people, you know, sexually."

"Why do you want that?"

"I don't know. It's just feelings I have inside."

"Just make them wear condoms if you're gonna do that."

"Alright, come here."

I was so ready, I didn't know what to do first. I pulled his jogging pants and boxers down to his ankles and put his dick in my hand. Already semi hard, it felt strange holding it in my hand. It looked like an alien with one eye. Something kept telling me to lick it, so I did. Jason stood on his tip toes. I didn't know what to do next, so I kept licking it like a Popsicle. I stopped and laid back on the bed.

Jason slid my panties off. When he got ready to push it in, I flinched. He pulled it back out. I reached down and felt his dick. The head was real wet. I thought it was blood, and looked at my hand. I saw that it wasn't blood. I grabbed his dick and put it to my cake entrance. He pushed into me slowly, sliding right in this time. It felt so good in there! He moved in and out. I moaned loud and then covered my mouth. Jason had his eyes closed. About four minutes later, my insides felt funny. It's an indescribable feeling. I began to tremble and a rush came over me. It went all the way down to my cake and felt like water gushed out. I know now that I had cum. It got even wetter down there. Jason did it harder and faster. I tried not to scream. The harder he did it, the more my cake made that wet noise. I felt the rush again. Jason breathing hard, pulled out of my cake, and came all over my cake hairs. That turned me on more. I reached for Jason's dick; he moved my hand away from it.

"Let's count the money," Jason said.

Jason left the room and came back with a warm bath cloth. I still lay there with my eyes closed when Jason walked back into the room. He wiped me down with a bath cloth. It felt so good when he ran the cloth across my lips, I couldn't help grabbing his finger and putting one in my cake. He moved it around. Damn, he pulled it out, licked his fingers, and started counting the money.

"Jason, what's wrong?" I asked.

"It's nothing."

"Don't tell me that, I know something is bothering you."

"I thought we were tight, but you want to fuck other guys."

"We are tight. It's not like I want to love them, I love you. It's just that my mind is always on different … you know … dicks, and I don't want to sneak and do it. I'm with you though, Jason, always."

"It is, what it is."

We got dressed and counted the money. It was $432,000.00.

"What are we gonna do with all of this money?" I asked.

"We are gonna invest it in something," Jason said.

"Like what?"

"What do you like to do?"

"Do I have to answer that?" I said, looking at his dick.

Jason shook his head and we burst out laughing.

"What about these packages?" I picked one of them up.

"I don't even know what that shit is."

"Can I open it?"

"No, that shit might be some deadly gas or some shit!"

"Or condoms."

"Shut up, girl, sex got your mind gone."

I soon left and went home. I didn't want Grandma smelling sex all on me, so I rushed to the bathroom. On my way there, I spotted my mama's picture and felt bad all over again.

Chapter 3

Jason

I don't know what the fuck has come over Arkeba. Since her mama's death, she has been on some crazy sex shit. Maybe she'll get over it, but in the meantime, I've got my own problems. I got all of this money, and I don't know how to invest this shit. I guess I'll just leave it in my closet until I think of something. My mama's laughter rang out from the living room and I thought about something. This is the first time that I have seen a man here all night, and the next day. I gotta find out what's up with this nigga, cause if he tries to play my mama, off with his head!

When I came out of my room, he was at the kitchen stove cooking, and my mama was watching TV. She wore a smile I've never seen before, as I walked past her to go outside.

"Come here, Jason!" she said in her Jamaican accent.

I didn't want to go back because I didn't want her to see this big ass gun sticking out from under my shirt. Johnny looked at me and winked, then said, "Leave that boy alone. Go ahead, little man."

"My name is Jason."

"How about I call you J-Money?"

I smiled at him. "That's cool."

I walked out the door onto the porch. Johnny soon followed with two plates of buffalo wings and French fries. He handed me a plate.

"So, why haven't you left my mama yet?" I asked.

"Should I have a reason to leave her?"

"No, she's a good person. Guys just don't stay around long."

"What if I told you that I'm in it for the long run?"

"You got a job?"

Johnny laughed at me. "No, I don't have a job yet. I'm looking, though. It's hard for a felon out here. You make sure you finish school, the streets don't love you."

"I'm not in the streets."

"The gun you got tucked says something different."

I covered my front so he couldn't see the gun.

"You can't hide that big ass gun, let me see it," Johnny said.

I pulled my gun out and handed it to him.

After Johnny got the gun in his hand, he pointed it to my head. "Empty your pockets, nigga!" he said through gritted teeth.

"Man, what…"

"Shut the fuck up and empty your pockets!"

I looked him in the eyes and took about four hundred dollars out of my pocket.

"If you're gonna shoot me, take me in the woods so my mama won't see it," I said, staring at him.

He smiled and gave me my gun back.

I didn't know what the fuck was going on.

"For future reference, never give somebody a gun to hold that you don't know or don't trust. In the streets, don't trust nobody, I mean nobody. That's how I ended up in the feds. I had one of the best black tar connects on the eastern part of North Carolina. Me trusting niggas cost me fifteen years of my life."

I took my gun out of his hand. Part of me wanted to shoot his ass for scaring me like that, but I respected his words. I never met my father, so I didn't know how to become a man. Keba was the closest one to me. Then I thought about what he said about the black tar.

"What's black tar?" I asked.

"It's heroin. That was my drug of choice to sell. You owe me a hundred dollars for not keeping your money."

I really didn't owe him shit, but I like Johnny, so I gave him a hundred.

"Do you ever think about getting back in the game?" I asked.

"No, but if I did, I would do shit a lot different."

"So what would it take for you to get back in the game?"

"You ask a lot of questions."

"I may be able to help."

"How can your little ass help me?"

"How much is a block of black tar this big and this thick?" I asked, showing him the measurement with my hands.

"That's about a key. It'll go for about $100,000."

My eyes grew big, but I couldn't tell Johnny I had three in the house.

"If it was broke down, how much could I make?"

"It depends on how good it is and how you step on it. I'll say if it's good, close to half a million."

"I came across some, and I want us to be partners."

Johnny looked at me for a second. "What kind of partners?"

"You know, I supply the stuff and you sell it."

"We'll need a spot and all that. Where your bad ass get a brick from?"

"I gotta go handle something, tell my moms I went down the street to play. Look for the spot, and I'll supply the money and dope!"

It was almost dark when the cab finally showed up at the store. I got in with my fitted pulled low. All the way across town, I asked myself if I could trust Johnny. I'm really concerned about what's going on with Arkeba though. My mind went from one point to another until I arrived at my destination. The cab dropped me off where I had a bike hidden in the bushes. I rode the bike to the street where Keba's mama was murdered. I watched a hooptie back up in the yard. I took my backpack off, went behind the house across from the spot, and quickly put on the skirt and halter top I had taken out of Keba's closet. I put tissue balls in the halter top as little breasts, skipped across the street like a little girl, and knocked on the door.

"Yo," someone said from behind the door, peeping through the peephole.

"Is my mama over here?" I asked in a little girl's voice.

A fat brown skin man opened the door. I put the .357 in his face, cutting him off. I heard two guys talking in the house.

"If you try anything, I will blow the front of your face out the back of your head!"

"Alright, little girl, or whatever you are, just chill!" He began to sweat.

"How many people are in here?" I asked.

"Besides me, two."

"Turn around and walk!" I whispered.

I walked behind him to the kitchen where one guy was bagging up heroin. The other guy had the kitchen counter stacked with money. He was brown skinned, with deep waves and a full beard.

"What the fuck!" the light skinned guy said.

I pushed the fat guy in the kitchen.

"Y'all line up on the wall over there!" I said, aiming the gun.

"Chill, lil nigga!" The brown skin guy said. "Do you know who spot this is? He will kill your whole family!"

"No, I don't, that's why I'm here to find out who spot it is. So who's gonna talk first?"

Nobody said anything. "Alright, since y'all don't want to tell me that, who killed Case?"

The guys looked at one another and still didn't say a word.

"I gotta get ready for school. I don't have time to play games with y'all!" I aimed my gun at the big man's head and pulled the trigger, blowing off half of his face. He was dead before he hit the floor.

"Oh shit... Oh shit!" both of the guys yelled.

"Who killed Case?"

"All we know is our lieutenant told us to hold her down, and he gave her the needle!" the brown skinned guy said. "We didn't know it would kill her!"

"Who is your lieutenant?" I asked, pointing the gun at the light skinned guy.

I didn't wait for him to answer. I pulled the trigger, sending a hole through his chest. The impact knocked him to the wall.

"Alright ... man, chill!" The brown skinned guy began to cry. "His name is Nitti!"

"Why did y'all kill her?"

"I don't know!"

"Good look!" I put the gun to his head and pulled the trigger. Blood splashed all over my face.

That shit made me hyper. I gave the light skinned guy another head shot. After stacking the heroin and money in my backpack, I eased out the back door. I skipped across the street, changed clothes back, got on my bike and rode away.

I called a cab about a mile from the scene. Johnny and my mama were gone when I walked in the house. I rushed to my room, grabbed a key of heroin, and stuffed it in the backpack with the money and other heroin. I took a shower, got dressed, and sat on the porch with the backpack beside me.

Thirty minutes later, Johnny and my mama pulled into the driveway. My mama got out the car, kissed me on the jaw, and went into the house. Johnny sat down beside me.

"What's good, J-Money?"

"Nothing, just waiting on you."

"For what?"

"Are we still gonna be partners?"

"Damn, I forgot about that. Yeah, what's up?"

I handed him the backpack. He opened it and looked around paranoid.

"Yo, what are you into, J-Money?"

"That's not important. Just know if you beat me, I will kill you."

Johnny started laughing. Jason reminded him of himself when he was young.

"Do you know where I can get more guns?" I asked.

"Yeah, I got you, where the other gun at?"

"Right here." I lifted my shirt.

"If you have done any dirt with it, take it in the woods and bury it, and never tell anyone where it's at."

I got up and ran straight to the woods. When I came back, Johnny was gone. I hope like hell he doesn't beat me. Tomorrow is Friday, damn I forgot tomorrow is my birthday. Let me go check on Keba.

I walked on the side of her house and the blocks were missing. A bike was parked beside Keba's window. A guy who looked like Puff Daddy's oldest son stood behind her, fucking her from the back. Keba looked at me, biting her bottom lip, trying to hold her moans in. She moved her lips, without sound, and told me she loves me. I didn't know if I should be hurt or what. I climbed off the bricks and went back home.

Johnny

I had to take a ride to clear my head. My son is on some other shit! Yeah, I said it right, Jason AKA Jay-Money is my son. I left my son and his mama for fifteen and a half years. Really, she was just one of my many women back then. Even though she claimed to hate me, in the whole fifteen and a half years, I got a letter from her every other week, sometimes every week. She sent pictures of her and Jason. She even sent money when my shit ran out. I didn't want to take food out of my son's mouth, but I was broke.

I had it all back in the day. That nigga, Man, set me up. The feds had certain conversations on me, me in pictures with heroin on the table, but Man was not in the pictures, and we were together almost every day. He fell in love with that white girl, Sarra. Neither one of them wrote me. The feds took all of my money, houses, everything except my car. Now, my fifteen-year-old son is putting me back on my feet. That's crazy, right? I'll do it right this time. I get caught again it's over. I gotta be extra careful.

Y'all may not believe me, but all of them Towns women are crazy! Towns is still a freak. I go over there to ask her about Case, and after she tells me, she turns toward me and bust her legs wide open. I see she still don't shave them fat pussy lips. Keba has grown a lot. The first thing she does is look at my dick print. She's still a damn baby. I hope Jason don't fall in love with her. If she is anything like her mama and grandmamma, she don't want no love, she only want dick. Now, there's Jean, Jason's mother. Oh, shit! The police are everywhere! I was going to see Big Dog. Yellow tape and police stood around the house. I stuffed the backpack under my passenger seat, parked on a side road and walked back to the scene. The ambulance workers were bringing three body bags out of the house.

I stopped and asked an old lady what happened. "I heard gunshots and looked out of my window. I didn't see anything strange. A little girl was playing in the street, then skipped down the road. That nice white car pulled up over there, and the next thing I know, child, police was pulling up everywhere," she explained.

She saw a detective coming our way, and walked off fast with her cane, back to her house, and closed the door. I walked to my car. By the looks of things, I won't be setting up shop at Big Dog's spot.

I rode around the corner and saw a little house. That spot could be a gold mine, and no one knew the secret to how I cut my heroin. I headed to my mama's house. I crept around back and stashed the heroin in her barn. It brought back so many memories. It was where I mixed my first batch of heroin. I could still see the stacks of money that I used to count on the table in the corner. Damn, I still haven't told Ma she got a grandson. I reached for the light switch and remembered Jason had asked me for some guns. I know I'm wrong for supplying him with guns, but he's accepted the streets. I'd rather he get caught with it, than without it. Judged by twelve than carried by six any day. Don't get me wrong, I'd rather he go to school and then college. He's already an A and B student. At the same time, I don't want to push him further into the streets.

I mashed the small button under the light switch. The wall slid back, and two of every kind of gun you can possibly name was bolted to the wall, still shiny. They may need a little oiling, but they're still ready to go. Jason didn't know, but I love guns too. I grabbed him a couple of 9's, 45's, and 38's, put them in a duffle bag, and walked out of the barn. When I opened the door, the wall automatically shut.

The lights were out when I pulled up in the driveway. I checked all the rooms. Jason was asleep on a mattress. I gotta get him a bed. He woke up when I was about to close the door.

"I thought you had dipped with the money and black tar," Jason said.

"You never have to worry about that again."

"Again?"

"I'll talk with you about that tomorrow, and there's somebody that I want you to meet."

I closed the door and went to Jean's room. She was asleep, naked, with her dildo beside her barely buzzing. I laughed, which woke her up her. Jean stretched; her dark nipples looked like large Hershey kisses.

"Did you tell him?"

"I'll tell him tomorrow."

I lay down and wondered half of the night where Jason had got the money and heroin from until I dozed off.

Man

I got out of my Benz, lost for words. How the fuck did I lose my connect, two of my workers, and my cousin in two damn weeks! I stood there watching them carry my auntie's only child out in a body bag. I remember his little red ass used to run through the house in his Batman drawers. I caught the tear before it fell from the corner of my eye. I'll cry after I catch the motherfucker that's responsible. Somebody is trying to destroy me. I need some good tight pussy to get my mind right. Just saying that made me think about good tight pussy Case. She had a pussy and ass that never got bigger. You go back and fuck her the next day, her shit was right back tight!

Damn, that looks like Johnny coming this way. When the fuck did he get out? I wonder if he got something to do with all of this killing shit. It can't be him; he would have come at me first. Maybe he's trying to make me suffer. My money is too long for him now. I'll just get somebody to off his ass. I watched him walk away, then I walked back to my car. Sarra laid back in the seat with ice in a towel on her lip. I buy this bitch anything she wants, and she still can't keep her mouth or legs shut. I flopped down in my car and she jumped.

"I just saw Johnny," I said.

"Johnny who?"

"Johnny that we set up with the feds."

"Oh shit, he's going to kill us!" Sarra said, looking out of the car windows,

"Bitch, shut up. That broke motherfucker can't pay attention."

"He damn sho can slang that big black monster dick!"

I backhanded that bitch in her eye! It swelled instantly.

"You keep fucking trying me, Sarra!"

"All I said was…"

I drew back to slap her ass again. She balled up by the door.

"Say it if you want to!" I yelled, pulling off.

Sarra is a pain freak. After I did all of that, the bitch went in her bra, pulled out an ecstasy pill, pulled her dress up, and slid it up her ass. She sat up, moved her ass around in the seat, then leaned over, unzipped my pants, pulled my dick out, and started to suck my dick head, then my dick. It's time I trade this bitch in for something young. Frank used to hook me up with all the young pussy. Now I gotta find my own. I wonder if Johnny knows that I set him up. Shit, it either was him or me. Fuck that nigga! I got six houses and two cars, with eight figures. I'm not going to jail if I can help it. This bitch don't even suck dick right no more. I'm not supposed be thinking about nothing but how good the shit feel, not no other shit. I went in my suit pocket and pulled my coke out. I took a hit up each nostril, as Sarra continued to suck my dick. It started going soft.

"What's wrong baby, I can't keep it up."

"Maybe it's time we go our separate ways."

"No, you will not leave me!" she yelled.

Y'all won't believe what that bitch did. While I was driving about sixty, she opened the car door and dove out of the car. I kept right on going. I didn't know if that bitch was dead or alive. I know she better find another ride home. Y'all can call me cold hearted, but shit, when the love is gone, it's gone! I pulled up in the driveway of my new baby mansion that I had built in Rocky Mount. Damn, I came a long way!

My butler came to meet me at the door.

"Go down the street and see if you see Sarra lying beside the road. If she is, take her stupid ass to the hospital."

My butler got in our company truck and left to look for Sarra.

All right, I still got a little love for the bitch.

Chapter 4

Arkeba

I woke up on top of the covers naked. My cake was a little sore, but I felt better, being that I had just lost my mama. I got up to take a shower for school. Ewww … that nasty nigga left two used condoms on the floor. I picked them shits up and flushed them down the toilet before Grandma saw them.

Today is Jason's birthday, and I haven't got him anything yet. I'll drive to the jewelry store to get him something this evening. That shit made me wet as hell, seeing Jason watch me getting fucked. I love Jason in my own special way.

After showering and getting dressed, I came out the door eating a Pop Tart. Jason stood there, waiting for me as usual. He was extra fly today. He wore a white Sean John button up with orange stripes, Sean John jeans, and orange and white Gortex boots. He topped it off with the chains he had taken from Frank.

"Happy birthday, baby!" I said and gave him a hug and a kiss on the lips.

"Thanks," he said, not hugging me back.

"Did I do something wrong?"

"Was the dick good?"

"It was all right, you should've told me that you were coming. I would've kept the pussy fresh for you. You come before anybody."

"Yeah, whatever!" He walked off toward school.

Walking behind him, I noticed he doesn't walk like a girl when he's mad. I burst out laughing. He looked back, rolled his eyes, and kept walking.

I met my friends at our usual spot at school. Most of the girls gathered around when they saw Jason. One yelled one... two... three ... They all sang happy birthday to him. He looked at me and smiled. I pulled him to me.

"Come over my house around 9:00 tonight. I got a big surprise for you," I whispered in his ear.

I kissed Jason on the lips and he walked off to his class. Grandma had told me that she was going out of town with her friend, and she wouldn't be back until Saturday morning so the car could pick us up for the funeral. We both were trying to occupy our time so we wouldn't go crazy.

In last period, I daydreamed about letting the white teacher fuck me. I rubbed my pussy through my capri pants until I got real wet. Before I could cum, the bell rang.

When Jason and I made it home from school, I went to my stash he had supplied me with, rushed back out of the house, got in my car and left. I wasn't neglecting Jason on his birthday, but I had to go buy him something. I know that he was still mad at me.

I parked on Main Street and walked to the jewelry store. The older white man was seeing a customer when I walked in. I had my back turned, looking at a diamond pinky ring. I turned around, and the man had his eyes glued to my ass. I smiled and pulled my good hair up into a long ponytail as he walked over.

"May I help you, I'm Chuck?" he asked.

"Can I look at that middle pinky ring?"

"Sure, anything you want," he said, looking me up and down.

I had to laugh at this old man flirting with me. He pulled the ring out and put it in my hand. I slipped it on my finger and looked at it.

"I'll take it!"
He went to the register and rang it up.
"That'll be $875.00."
"Can I get it gift wrapped, please?"
"No problem, do you want it engraved?"
"Yes."
"What shall I put?"
"My name is Arkeba Kenyatta Towns, just put, Love, AKT."

Chuck stared at me with his mouth wide open. Then raced to the back. He came back with the box gift wrapped and handed it to me. He never took the money, and I wasn't about to remind him. I thanked him and walked out of the jewelry store. How strange was that?

I went to Walmart and bought Jason and me a cell phone with the money I kept for the ring. On my way out of the electronics section, I passed some camcorders on sale. I decided to buy one for the surprise I have for Jason tonight.

On the way home, I stopped by the store and paid a wino to go in the store and get me a six pack of strawberry daiquiris. My mama used to love them when I was a little girl. That made me miss my mama. I pulled in Tracy's driveway and blew the horn. She stayed a block from the store. Tracy is brown skinned, seventeen years old, 5'7", 135 pounds, shoulder length hair, and hazel brown eyes. That's my girl from school. She came out of the house in a white tank top, short brown khaki shorts, and white sandals.

"Who car you got, girl?" Tracy asked.

"Mine, I think my daddy bought it for me, and I don't even know who he is or how he looks."

"Well, we know that he's not black, that's for damn sure."

We burst out laughing. My mind went to her cake print. I tried to shake it out of my head. I just wondered how much different her pussy was from mine. This is my girl; I'll tell her my thoughts later. She probably is thinking the same shit. We rode around for a while.

"Your grandmother will be home for the funeral, right?" Tracy asked.

"She won't miss her only daughter's go away for the world."

"I didn't tell my mama she wasn't gonna be home."

"We gonna party tonight!"

"Do you remember what you asked me to do?"

"Yeah."

"Well, I gotta tell you the truth, I'm still a virgin."

I was shocked, as much as she talks about sex.

"We gotta do something about that fat pussy then, don't we?" There I said it.

Tracy burst out laughing and started dancing to my Double L mix CD.

Jason

Where the hell did Arkeba go? She done got on some real freak shit. I kind of like that shit though. Today is my sixteenth birthday. I heard a horn blowing and I went to the door. Who the fuck? I opened the door. A 2002 White Honda Accord was parked beside Johnny's Corvette.

My mama yelled, "Surprise!" She kissed me on the jaw and wished me a happy birthday. She and Johnny had bought me a car. I ran to the car, hopped in, and turned the radio on. They had a lot of music installed in my car. Johnny walked to the driver side window.

"I would've got you rims, but the shit we're about to do, you don't need the heat. Gone and take it around the block. When you come back, I need you to take a ride with me," Johnny said.

I cranked the car up and drove around the block smiling. I passed Keba in her car. She saw that it was me, turned around, and blinked her headlights behind me. Keba pulled up beside me after I came to a stop.

"Boy, who car you got?" Keba asked.

"Hey, Jason!" Tracy said.

"What's up? It's mine, Johnny and my mama got it for my birthday."

"That's what's up, are you still coming over tonight?"

"Yeah, so there is no need for no niggas to be there, right?"

"No, baby, I'll see you then."

I pulled off, turning my system up. I got to find that nigga, Nitti. I'll chill tonight, but best believe I'm going hunting for his ass tomorrow.

Johnny was waiting for me when I got back to the house. We got in his Vette and left.

"I decided to buy a trap house in Pinetops. That's the town over," Johnny said.

"I know where it's at, but why not have one in Tarboro?"

"That shit hot right now. We don't need the extra heat. So while you go to school, me and my people down here gonna get this shit jumping. We'll get a spot in Tarboro later."

"Why are you so good to me and my mama? She seems so happy."

"I might as well go ahead and tell you now."

"Tell me what … you leaving her ain't you!" I almost yelled.

He took a deep breath. "I'm your real father."

I was lost for words. Johnny glanced at me. Tears started falling down my face. I use to always ask God why I don't have a daddy.

"It's okay, I won't leave you again. If I do, it'll be for taking care of you and your mama."

I wiped my eyes. I couldn't tell him about the murders yet. I kept quiet all the way to Pinetops. Inside, I was smiling, happy that I was finally with my daddy. Boy, what a birthday gift.

Pinetops only has three stop lights and a couple stores. That's the best way that I can describe it. We drove in the front yard of an old wooden house. It looked like it was built in the 1800's. An older man came out of the house. He was bald-headed and skinny, wearing a white short sleeved button up, black dress pants, and black dress shoes. A black 1985 Oldsmobile Cutlass sat in the front yard. He pimped to Johnny's car. Johnny and I got out of the car to meet him. He shook hands with Johnny and stared at me, then looked at my gun sticking out from under my shirt.

"Who is this lil nigga?" he asked Johnny.

"This is my son, Jason. Jason, this is Tiny."

"I didn't know you had a son," Tiny said. "Y'all come in."

Johnny went back to the car and got the heroin. He had put his special cut on it already. By the time we got through bagging shit up, it was 7:30. My hands were killing me, but once that first customer came and tested the dope, I was happy. Johnny handed me my first $50.00 off the heroin. We got in the car and left. Johnny drove around the corner and pulled into a yard. He handed me a key.

"What's this for?" I asked.

"This will be our stash house."

We went into the house. Johnny carried a tote bag. He emptied the guns and heroin on the kitchen table. My eyes lit up, seeing those guns.

"Always keep a gun at the spot, and plenty at the stash spot. Follow me."

I followed Johnny in the backroom. He took the tote bag, pulled up a square in the floor, put the bag in, and closed it. It was digital and locked on its own. Johnny handed me the digital code on a piece of paper.

"No one knows about this house, but me and you. Never bring no one here with you, and never tell anyone about it," Johnny said, walking out the door and back to the car.

On the way home, I felt like talking.

"Johnny, why you never wrote me or let my mama bring me to see you?"

"Ask your mama, she can explain that. But whatever she says, don't be mad at her, alright?"

"Can you ... never mind."

"You can ask or talk to me about anything, what's up?"

"I'm looking for this guy named Nitti, I got a score to settle with him."

"I don't know him, but I'll find him for you. Whatever you're doing, be careful."

I rubbed my gun in my lap and put my feet on the twin 9's I had in the brown paper bag on the floor.

We made it back to Tarboro, and Johnny drove around the corner from where I had shot the three guys.

"See that house right there?" Johnny said, pointing, "We are renting that house too. That's where we will have our other spot at after we get things up and running.

"So we gonna have two spots?"

"This is just the beginning, we're gonna get rich. We gotta go somewhere else."

Johnny pulled into a driveway, where an older lady sat on the porch, with Betty Wright's "First Time," playing low.

"Come on," Johnny said, getting out of the car.

I followed him to the house. The closer I got to the lady, the more I noticed that looked like her. She put her hand to her chest when she saw me, and her eyes watered up. She was my complexion, about 5'6," with short salt and pepper hair.

"Come here, baby," she said, opening her arms.

I walked into her arms. I felt so safe there. I hugged her back tight; she let me go and started hitting Johnny.

"Why…you…didn't…tell…me…about my…grandbaby!"

Johnny ducked and ran away laughing. It made me laugh. She took my hand and guided me into the house. She showed me my granddaddy, all the pictures of Johnny when he was little, and pictures of some of Johnny's old girlfriends. She cut me a big piece of her strawberry cake. This was the best cake I ever tasted in my life. She and I talked for about an hour. Johnny was ready to go, so I promised her that I would visit again soon.

When we made it back to the house, Johnny and I both had that happy look. My momma sat on the porch drinking a Heineken.

"Where the hell y'all been?" she asked.

"We been doing us, and I took him to see his grandmother," Johnny said.

"You told him!" She smiled at us.

"Yeah, why you didn't tell me, or take me to see him?" I asked with an attitude.

"Because he was a cheater and I was being selfish. I couldn't stand him, and I was afraid you would like him more than me and leave me by myself."

"Ma, I would never leave you." I wiped her tears away and kissed her on the cheek.

I went to my room to stash my guns. My mattress was gone off the floor and I had a whole new bedroom set, nightstand, all of that! I saw an envelope on the nightstand with my mama's handwriting on it. It was a birthday card with $20.00 inside. It said *Mommy loves you*. I rubbed the handwriting and dropped a tear. I had my family together.

Arkeba

"Where the hell is this damn boy at?" I said.

"He needs to come on," Tracy added.

Tracy and I had drank two daiquiris each while we sat in the front room waiting for Jason. We had the front room filled with birthday decorations. I looked out the window and saw Jason coming toward my house. He knocked on the door. Tracy and I rushed in the hallway, so he couldn't see us. I yelled for him to come in. Jason walked into the house and closed the door.

A kitchen chair sat in the middle of the living room. I pressed play on the remote. Uncle Luke from 2 Live Crew screamed, "Shake that ass, pump that pussy, doo-doo brown!"

I walked out in a bra and G-string and guided Jason to the chair. Tracy hid out of sight, recording me. I began to give him a lap dance. His dick felt like it was gonna burst out of his pants as I grinded hard against him. I stood up and stripped for him. After I was naked, I unbuttoned his shirt and pulled it off. Leaning down, I whispered in his ear.

"Happy birthday, baby, I'll be right back!"

I went to the hallway and took the recorder from Tracy. I changed the CD to "Slow Motion," by Juvenile.

Tracy danced her way to Jason, in her bra and G-string. He smiled and licked his lips. She danced even nastier than me. Shit, she made my cake wetter! This bitch can't be a virgin. She turned around, bent all the way over in Jason's face, and pulled her G-string down. I had to get closer on this. I zoomed in on her pussy in Jason's face. He spread her butt cheeks and rubbed her pussy. Tracy danced away from him, took her bra off, and threw it in his lap. I couldn't take it anymore! My hand went to my cake, as I recorded them. She grabbed Jason's hand and pulled him to my room. I followed behind them with the recorder. Tracy climbed on the bed and opened her legs like I taught her.

Jason kicked his shoes off and pulled his pants and boxers down at the same time. He got on the bed, kissed Tracy's lips lightly, then kissed her forehead. Jason kissed down to her nipples, then sucked on one, then the other. Tracy laid under him breathing hard with her mouth wide open. He went down Tracy's stomach, leaving little kisses. Jason skipped her cake and kissed down her leg. He kissed one toe at a time, back up her other leg, all the way to her hip. Jason went down to her cake lips. Tracy couldn't be still. Damn, she got a fat clit! Jason spread her lips open and her clit came out further. He moved his tongue lightly over her clit.

Tracy arched her back. "Oh ... oh my ... God!"

Jason licked her clit until she grabbed the sheets and yelled my name. Jason stopped. Tracy had wet my sheets. She laid there with her eyes closed, moaning. Jason aimed his dick at her pussy. She opened her eyes and handed him the condom from under the pillow. Tracy would not look at his dick. Jason finally got the condom on. I zoomed in on Tracy's face as he tried to enter her. Tracy screamed her ass off! Jason finally got the head in. He pushed about four inches in, and she screamed so loud, I thought somebody would call the police. Jason didn't move until Tracy calmed down. She wrapped her arms around him. He pushed all the way in. Tracy held him tight. Jason moved in and out of her slowly.

"OH … OH … AH … AH … OH!" she moaned.

They went at it missionary style for ten minutes. Jason made a face that I've only seen when he's about to cum. I zoomed in on his face as he filled the condom. Blood was all over the condom and my sheets. Tracy rolled over and lay there. I zoomed in on the wet blood spot that was on her leg. She got up and went to the bathroom. I had already run her some hot bubble bath water before Jason came. I took Jason's condom off and followed Tracy to the bathroom. I came back with a wet washcloth and washed Jason off. Once he was clean and smelling like soap, I set the camcorder on the dresser so it could record us. I lay between Jason's legs and put his dick in my mouth, moving up and down. Jason made a face like I was hurting him, so I stopped. I just sucked the head and jacked his dick. He reached down and rubbed my hair. I kept doing it until he was all the way hard.

Tracy walked in my room, with a towel wrapped around her. She grabbed the camcorder and got closer.

"It's big!" Tracy said. "I took all of that!"

I let Jason's dick go, got on top of him, and squatted down on his dick. I moved down slow. Damn almighty! Tracy zoomed in on me going down on it. I had never rode before, but it felt good going in. I went all the way down and hopped my ass up fast. I was riding Jason, with half of it in me and he had me moaning. Jason moaned with me. He came up to meet me, pushing it all in. Jason held me tight so I wouldn't run. I screamed and moaned. He was tearing my cake up. I felt myself cumming. It ran out of me, down his balls. I hopped up and jacked his dick until his cum shot all over my face. I heard Tracy say, "Oh my God!"

"Please tell me you got that!" I said to Tracy, licking Jason's cum off of my lips.

"Girl, you're a trip!" Tracy laughed. "I got that!"

Tracy and I took Jason to the bathroom and bathed him. We drank the rest of the wine coolers and went at it again until we all fell asleep.

I woke up the next morning on one side of Jason and Tracy on the other. I had to go pee. When I came back in the room, Tracy was holding Jason's dick in her hand looking at it while he slept. I heard a car pulling up. I looked out of the window. It was Grandma! I pulled Jason half way off the bed by his arm.

"Boy, my grandma out there!" I said.

Jason jumped up. I pushed him all the way out the back door, with his clothes in his hands. I had forgotten his gifts, so I ran to my room, got the gifts, and ran back to the back door. Jason was stepping into his pants on the back porch. I handed him the two wrapped gifts, gave him a kiss, and closed the door. I ran back to my room. Tracy had put on a nightgown. I slipped on my nightgown and met Grandma at the door. Soon as Grandma walked in the house, she started sniffing the air. Grandma went from room to room, sniffing until she got to my room. She opened my room door. Tracy lay on my bed like she was asleep. Grandma took two deep sniffs, then closed my door.

"Get ready so we can go to the funeral home," Grandma said. "And Keba, I can smell cum a mile away!" She slammed her door.

I ran to my room. Tracy lay on my bed with her eyes bucked open and her hand over her mouth. After hearing Grandma, Tracy was scared! I covered my mouth to keep from laughing. I looked at the clock, then Tracy and I ran to the bathroom. I wanted to block this out like it didn't happen to my mama. I didn't want my mama to be dead.

The family car pulled up. Grandma, Tracy, and I got in the car wearing all black. I was so scared! I grabbed Tracy's hand and held it tight. She squeezed my hand to let me know that she was there.

I saw Jason, his mom, and Johnny getting in his car. I yelled for the driver to stop, rolled down the window, and screamed Jason's name. He looked back in his black suit. The pinky ring that I bought him gleamed on his hand.

"I need you, please ride with us!" I cried.

Johnny told him to go ahead. Jason walked fast to the limo and got in beside me. Grandma stared at him, then at Tracy and me.

The funeral was packed. People really did love my mama. That alone brought tears to my eyes. We were escorted to the front row. The eulogy seemed to go on forever. The choir sang four songs, and then it was time to go see my mother for the last time. The casket was open; I began to scream for my mama. Jason held me tight. A white man walked up … wait, was this the white man at the jewelry store? He dropped a diamond ring in my mama's casket on the sly. Maybe I'm seeing things. Jason helped me up. I built the courage to go to her casket. Mama looked so peaceful laying there. I pushed her hair behind her ear like she used to do me.

"I love you, Mama, rest in peace," I cried.

Jason escorted me out of the funeral home. I didn't stop looking back until her casket was out of sight. We went to the burial and returned to Grandma's house to eat. A caterer was there and served everybody the prepared meal of fried chicken, candied yams, greens, cornbread, and coleslaw. A light-skinned man in all white showed up at our house with a young light skinned girl on his arm. She looked about eighteen or nineteen years old, and her hair was long on one side and shaved on the other. She had the biggest lips I have ever seen on a person. I imagined her mouth wrapped around my cake hole. Grandma stared at him as he walked up to us.

"Towns, I'm so sorry to hear about Case," the man said.

Grandma shook her head up and down. He leaned over and whispered in her ear, but I could still hear him.

"Call me later. I'll make you feel better."

Grandma slapped blood in the corner of his mouth. He pulled his handkerchief out and wiped his mouth.

"Leave!" Grandma yelled.

Johnny came up beside me and Grandma, and Jason followed. They both stared at the man with murder in their eyes.

"Oh, y'all back together?" he said, then walked off laughing, with the girl behind him.

I thought to myself, *back together?* From the look on Jason's face, he was probably thinking the same thing. After the man left, everybody went back to eating. I have some questions for Grandma when these people leave.

Man

I can't believe that old bitch put her hands on me. I would kill her ass if it wasn't for her helping me to become the man that I am. I gotta go see Sarra at the hospital today. She was run over by another car when she jumped out of my car. I gotta drop this little bitch off first. She's eighteen years old, with a pussy the size of a porn star. I pulled up in front of her house, and she had the nerve to lean over and try to kiss me. If her pussy is that big, I can only imagine what them big lips has accomplished. I turned my head. She popped her mouth and got out.

Twenty minutes later, I pulled in front of the emergency room, put a handicap sign in the window, and got out. My mind kept telling me, *fuck this bitch, just leave,* but she got one of them pussies and assholes that fit my dick perfectly. I pushed the button on the elevator, thinking about fucking Sarra right there on the hospital bed. The elevator came open. I walked into her room with my dick getting harder and harder.

When I pushed the door open, two white detectives stood there in suits. Sarra's bed was empty. The short detective walked toward me with an evil look on his face.

"I'm Detective Smith, and this is my partner, Detective Ham. Your name is Man, right?" he asked.

"Why?"

"Is your real name Donald Brown?" Detective Ham asked.

"Yes, where is Sarra?"

Detective Smith grabbed me and put me in a wrestling move, then slammed me to the floor on my face.

"You are under arrest for the murder of Sarra Moore."

"I didn't murder anybody. She jumped out of my car!"

They snatched me up off the ground. My face had started to swell.

"Tell it to the judge!" Detective Ham said as he read me my rights.

They shoved me all the way to their detective car. Once I was in the car, they called me every kind of nigga one could think of.

We arrived at the police station. The two detectives took me straight to the interrogation room and slammed me into a chair.

"Why did you do it?" Detective Smith yelled.

"Fuck you, call my lawyer!"

Detective Smith ran toward me. Detective Ham grabbed him and pushed him out of the interrogation room. I had seen this on TV so many times until I laughed and started clapping. The good cop and bad cop were good to watch, until Detective Ham went into his pocket, pulled out a recorder, and pressed play. Someone could be heard asking another person to state their name. A groggy voice said, "Sarra Moore."

I hopped up out of my seat.

"That's not Sarra!" I screamed.

Detective Ham looked at the thick tinted glass. "Turn the TV on, and press play," he said.

The TV came on in the corner. Sarra lay in the hospital bed with her whole body swollen. I felt bad for her; we had been through so much together. Then I heard the detective ask, "Who did this to you?"

Sarra swallowed hard, then said, "Man ...push ... me ... out ... car."

"Ma'am ... hold on a little longer ..." Detective Smith said, wiping his eyes as he stood beside her, holding her hand.

"What's his real name?"

Sarra began to cry. "Don ... ald Brow ... nn," she said, just loud enough to be heard.

Her body began to convulse and I closed my eyes.

Detective Hamm grabbed my jaws and squeezed.

"Look at her, motherfucker!" he screamed.

I stared straight at the TV until Sarra's body went limp and the monitors flatlined. I dropped my head on the table. I just knew I was fucked, even though I didn't do it. But with one of the best lawyers in the eastern district, anything stood a chance of being beaten. Just to think, I had feelings for that bitch.

The detectives took me to the magistrate's office and gave me a million dollar bond. I looked at the two detectives and smiled. They picked me up by the elbows and dragged me off to jail. After waiting for almost two hours, I was finally given my call. My lawyer was on a three million dollar retainer for times like this. He made a couple of calls, and I was out the door in three hours. Before I made it to my auntie's car, Detectives Smith and Ham met me, smiling and holding up a warrant.

"We towed your Benz and got a search warrant," Detective Smith said.

Damn, I forgot about the seven grams of coke I had been getting high off of, and the gun under my seat. I dropped my head and turned around to be cuffed. This shit could go federal! I cried on my way back in the jail. Once I got back, I called my lawyer and told him what happened. All he said was he'll get to it first thing Monday morning. I hung up and called my lieutenant.

"Code 3," was all I said. It meant to clear everything out of all the houses and take the money to Auntie.

My lieutenant didn't say a word, just like I taught him. He hung up and got to work.

The jailers ordered me to squat and cough. That's the most

embarrassing shit of my life! Bending over and letting another man look in my ass. I finally got dressed in a damn orange jumpsuit, and old ass shower shoes. They opened the cellblock and musk, shit, and weed odor smacked me dead in the face! I felt like throwing up! Most of the guys called my name. Some even offered me their rooms. I ended up rooming with a guy the feds had got for conspiracy, from Ahoskie, North Carolina. After putting the sheets on the thin ass mattress, I had to lay down. I was determined to sleep until Monday.

Grandma Towns

I'm glad all them people done got out of my damn house. That damn Man has always been an emotional little bitch! I taught that motherfucker everything he knows, and he gonna try to handle me? But I got something for his ass! I'll get the last laugh! I know y'all are wondering how I came in contact with Johnny and Man. I might as well tell y'all. Listen well, because I won't repeat this shit again, not even to my grandbaby.

I decided to go to the club one night. I was about twenty-eight years old back then. I had the body of a goddess, and from what I've been told, the fattest pussy any of the men I've been with have ever seen. I remember it like it was yesterday. I walked in the club in a black catsuit and black high heels. My hair hung to my ass, and my pussy stuck out like a heavyweight boxers closed fist. All the men chose me, but I determined who got this pussy. Besides, I was on a mission tonight. I was fucking this white man, who had plenty of money, and coke for days. I thought he was gonna break me off for giving him the pussy. This mother fucker gave me one hundred dollars, like some damn hooker! This pussy is golden, baby, you gotta pay to play! He ended up getting hooked on the pussy but was stingy with his money.

I soon learned his operation inside and out. I didn't know that he always had me followed. Shit, he couldn't make me cum like I wanted to, so I gave my baby daddy the pussy when I wanted a couple of good nuts. He had him killed and he beat my ass. How could I explain that shit to Cassandra?

Anyway, I walked through the club and went straight to the bathroom. I saw two young guys on the side of the wall smoking a joint. It smelled so damn good, I asked them to hit it. They handed it to me. After hitting the joint, they told me they were 17 years old, and their names were Johnny and Man. I went and bought them a drink, and then we danced a couple of songs. After the dance, they followed me back to our seats, like a puppies follow their mother. They were well mannered. These were the guys I was looking for. I whispered in their ears that I wanted to get out of there. They looked at each other, smiled like little boys, and followed me out of the club. I asked them what they were driving. Johnny pointed to an old rusty Ford pickup truck. I wasn't riding in that shit! They followed me in my red Cougar to the hotel.

Once we got in the room, I went to the bathroom and came out naked. They stood there with their mouths open, staring at how fat my pussy was. I had to tell them to take their clothes off. I knew then that they were virgins. Man had a ten-inch dick, but that damn Johnny was hung like a damn horse, and it was fat! Shit, I was scared of his young ass, but I had to play it off. I lay on the bed and called Johnny to my face. I told Man to put it in my pussy. Man got on top of me and couldn't find the hole. I had to let Johnny's dick go, and guide him in me. Once Man was in, he started breathing hard. I grabbed Johnny's dick and put that big motherfucker in my mouth. I only could get half of it in there, and my mouth was stretched to the max.

Man fucked me like a jack rabbit. It felt good though. I moaned while sucking Johnny's dick. Before we got started good, they both were cumming. Man pulled out and came all over my pussy hairs. Johnny stood on his tiptoes, cursing, as I sucked all the cum out of his dick. I got up, went to the bathroom, and washed off. I was ready for round two. I walked out of the bathroom, climbed between Man's legs, and put his dick in my mouth. I put my ass in the air and told Johnny to put it in. He got behind me and pushed that dick in me. When I tell y'all that young nigga had my pussy spread open, God damn! He was so deep in me, my stomach poked out every time he went in. I barely could keep Man's dick in my mouth.

Johnny started drilling my pussy! I tried to slide away from him. He held my hips and pounded as I screamed for dear life. I came so hard, I farted and dropped down to the bed. How about that young nigga followed me to the bed, and kept pounding my pussy, until I came again. Boy, was I glad for that break! Johnny, Man, and I fucked in so many positions. After that night, I had them eating out of my hand. Johnny and I had got closer. Man always had some bullshit going on with him. All right, damn, it was because of Johnny's dick also. Y'all bitches know how it is. Man still got the pussy when I wanted him to have it.

We messed around for years until I saw them at my daughter's house. I cut their asses off for a while, but two dicks like that were just hard to let go. I had to set an example for my grandbaby, so I had to slow down. So, now y'all know what's up. I know y'all are talking shit about me. Kiss my ass, shit. I won't tell y'all any more because I'm not incriminating my damn self. Just know, I did what I had to do, so my baby wouldn't go hungry or want for shit. Damn, I miss my baby so much. I wonder if Johnny and Man ran a train on my baby. Damn, Arkeba is knocking at my door, and my pussy wet.

"Come in, baby!" I yelled.

I already knew that she was gonna question me. Just looking at her damn white skin made me smile, 'cause I had taught her mama to juice white men.

"Why are you smiling, Grandma?" Keba asked.

"No reason, just thinking about how pretty you are."

"What was that man talking about?"

"Johnny and I used to be real close friends, so everyone thought we were a couple."

"How did you meet him?"

"We met at a club a long time ago."

"Okay," Keba said and left the room.

I know she didn't believe me, but I don't give a damn. I'm the adult and she's the child. Now I would be wrong if I asked her why my damn house smelled like cum! She got sneaky ways just like her mama. Damn, I miss my baby. I wonder who could hurt such a pretty girl. I heard Keba running to her ringing cell phone. Telling y'all about Johnny and Man done made me want some dick. I gotta call my old man; he's giving me some more of that dick tonight.

Jason

That nigga, Man, is really trying to die. I wonder what all that shit was about. Time will tell, though.

Johnny and I pulled up at the spot in Pinetops. Junkies were lined up at the front door. We had to go around the back. Tiny came to the door with a .44 long barrel in his hand. The damn gun was almost his height.

"Come on in, my son is in the back," Tiny said.

I went to the back room. A dark skinned guy about my age, with a birthmark on his jaw, was counting money. He took his fitted hat off and scratched his six-inch dreads.

"What's good, my pops told me about you. I'm Lil' T," he said and handed me a blunt.

"I'm Jason. What's good, you need some help with that?" I hit the blunt and pushed it back.

"I'm just finishing up."

"It's you and your pops' shift now," Lil' T. said, getting up and stretching.

Y'all wouldn't believe the money that was coming through that little ass town. We were getting the shit off so fast that Johnny had sent me to the stash spot twice. We never kept over $10,000 in the spot, and only as much heroin as we could put in the bucket of acid beside the door if the police came. The shit was fun at first, until Johnny sat me down and told me that we needed to talk. I was feeling a little buzz from the weed.

"This is not a game. People will kill you over this shit and money. Whatever you do, don't make a career out of this shit or the shit that you're doing. I want you to go to college and become somebody."

"I got you. I won't let you down, all right. Just take care of my mama while I'm away."

"You don't have to worry about that as long as I'm alive," Johnny said. "So, what's up with you and Keba?"

"That's my best friend."

"You haven't hit that?"

"Men don't tell everything, right?"

Johnny looked at me and smiled. He knew what was up. He'd seen me leaving her house this morning, and he acted like he didn't see me sneaking in our back door.

Before we knew it, two o'clock in the morning had hit, and Tiny and Lil' T were coming through the door. I was tired as shit. On the way home, my mind began to roam. I had to run my thoughts by Johnny.

"Hey, Johnny." He turned his radio down and looked at me. "Why we got to work in the spot? Why we can't just pay some workers to handle that?"

"We don't have the money to pay workers yet."

"I got money to pay the workers, then we can just let Tiny and Lil' T pick the money up and drop the stuff off. You can trust him that much, can't you?"

"Yeah, we go way back. He never showed me no grimy shit. I do this and bring you with me so that I can keep an eye on you. Where did you get this money and heroin from anyway?"

"I got it. That's all that matter, and I got two more keys of heroin."

Johnny hit the brakes and stopped in the middle of the road.

"Where did you get all that shit from, Jason?" he yelled. "I hope you haven't put our lives in jeopardy!"

"We're good, Johnny. Chill!"

Johnny pulled off in deep thought.

"I got in touch with my connect. We are back in with him too. When we get through with the three, we'll be ready to rock. Let's do this whole one, then we'll put people in the spot and open the one up in Tarboro."

"Did you check—"

"Yes, I'll have something for you on Nitti by Monday when you get out of school."

We pulled into the driveway. I called Arkeba as soon as I got out of the car, but she didn't answer, so I went to her house. The bricks were under her window again. I climbed up and looked through the window. This girl had blanked. A dyke chick who looked like a guy, with breasts and a fat ass fucked Keba from the back with a dildo. The chick laid the dildo down and slid the strap-on in place.

Keba turned to the side, and she fucked her hard. They changed position, and I watched Keba slide the dildo into her pussy with her back facing the chick. Keba rode the dildo like it was the best dick she ever had. She opened her eyes and jumped a little when she saw me. As sweat dripped off her body, she smiled and blew a kiss at me. Keba continued to ride, and even leaned back to open her cake lips so I could see the dildo going in and out of her pussy.

I was gonna watch all of this. I couldn't believe Keba, but my dick was cement hard. The dyke chick must have cum because her body went limp. Keba kept going. She rode the dildo and stared into my eyes until she came. I eased off the bricks and went home.

Johnny was up waiting for me. "We gotta talk, let's go outside," he said. I followed him outside and we sat on the porch chairs. "I've been thinking since we had our talk in the car. Maybe you should let me handle the illegal shit, and you go to school, then college so we can clean this money up."

"Why can't I help you?"

"You'll be helping me by going to school, and I'll make sure that you get your proper money. Trust me, son, this shit is not really for you."

"Alright, whatever."

I went in the house, got a pillowcase, put the two keys of heroin and $50,000 inside, and brought it to Johnny.

"See, this the shit I'm talking about. You got all this shit where we lay our head at. You got to be wiser than that. Monday, we are going to talk to a lawyer so you can clean up the money you got left, cause I know you didn't give me your last."

"Whatever, Daddy!" I said and walked into the house.

I was tired. Soon as my back hit the bed, I was out.

Chapter 6

Man

Monday Morning

Y'all won't believe how happy I am that today is Monday. My lawyer got to get me the fuck out of here today. I'm tired of niggas snoring, stinky feet, and bad breath. All this jail shit is crazy. These slaveholders gotta kill me to get me back in jail after this! They fed us some shit yesterday that these niggas call 'shit on the shingle.' How you gonna eat something with that name? I got my tray and looked at it closely. It really looked like tiny shit balls in some gravy. I like to threw up. Fuck that, I'm good! The jailer busted the door open with an attitude. If I had to smell this shit every day, I would be mad too. He was in his late thirties, white, fat, and medium height, with the smallest nose I have ever seen on a grown person.

"Brown, you got a legal visit!" he said with a frown.

I hopped off my bunk and almost ran out of the block. The jailer escorted me to a small room, where my lawyer sat twisting a gold pin in his hand. He stood up and shook my hand.

"How are you holding up?" Tommy asked.

"When are you going to get me out of here?" I blurted out before I sat down.

"I got some good news and some bad news. Which one do you want first?"

"Stop the bullshit, Tommy!"

"The good news is they can't charge you with the drugs and the gun. The warrant had your name on it, but the car is not in your name, and they didn't see you driving it, so it is an illegal search."

"That means I'm free to go, right?"

"No, that pissed the judge off. He wants you nailed to the cross. So happens that Sarra's uncle is a retired judge, who all the judges have a great deal of respect for. The judge came off your bond."

"Where was he when I took care of Sarra's homeless ass for the last sixteen years? So what now?" I asked.

"I've spoken with the DA. He said, being that you don't have a record and have cooperated on numerous occasions with the feds, he'll give you a deal if you cop out to involuntary manslaughter."

"And how much time is that?"

"Three to five years."

"Three to five years! I can't do that shit!"

"Listen, not as your attorney, but as a friend, this is good as it's gonna get. The retired judge is trying to get it pushed up to second-degree murder. The faster we enter the plea and get you in front of a judge, the better."

"I didn't push her out of my car!"

"Her statement on camera, her dying on camera, the detective crying. Picture how the jurors are gonna look at that, even if you didn't do it."

"Where do I sign?"

Tommy handed me the papers. I signed them with tears running down my face. I gave this cracker three million dollars, and I still got to sign my life away for three years. For some shit I didn't even do! I hope that bitch wake up and die again!

Without another word, I got up and knocked on the door. The

jailer opened the door and I walked out without even looking back at my lawyer. I had done all that snitching for the feds, and now the same people that I helped are sending my ass back to prison. Soon as I got back to the block, they called me right back out for my first appearance.

On the ride to court, I looked to my left and saw the two houses that I own. We soon passed by the strip that I run. I sat in the back of the sheriff van in handcuffs that were master locked to a chain around my waist and shackles around my ankles. Now y'all tell me this ain't some slave shit! I stepped out of the van and cameras flashed in my face. I couldn't cover up because my hands were chained around my waist.

The jailers met me at the entrance door with the other jailers and rushed me into the courtroom.

After my lawyer explained that we would rather skip all delays, and set a date for my plea, the judge set the date for three months from today. I looked back and saw Nitti and Auntie sitting in court. I felt so embarrassed with all of those chains and shackles on me. I dropped my head and walked back out of the courtroom. On the way back to jail, I turned my neck from right to left, hoping to see someone I knew. Shit, I got enough money to hold me down until I die. I just hate that I'm going to prison for something I didn't do. As they say, what goes around comes around two times.

Chapter 7

Jason

Keba and I still walked to school together. She talked about getting her license and how that dyke chick gave her so many nuts that she almost passed out. The loud I had rolled and smoked on my way to school made me laugh even louder at her crazy ass. Keba acted like she was mad because I wouldn't stop laughing.

On the way to my locker, it seemed like everyone was staring at Keba and I. Tracy walked toward us. I had to smile at her pretty ass. She walked up to me and tongued me down. Everyone looked at Keba, wondering if she was going to do anything. Keba turned my face toward hers and tongue kissed me also. She then grabbed Tracy and tongued her down as well.

Tracy wasn't expecting that, and she backed away from Arkeba. "What the fuck are you doing?" Tracy asked.

"You want to show people that you got the dick, instead of keeping it on the low. Well, I showed them that I can get your pussy!"

Tracy burst out laughing. "Bitch, you're crazy. I love you, though!"

I walked off, shaking my head.

In my first four hours at school, I'd collected five numbers. While trying to stay awake in history class, I noticed Keba at the door motioning for me to come out. I got a bathroom pass and met her in the hallway.

"What's good?" I asked.

"Go to the girls' bathroom," Keba said.

I went and stood in front of the bathroom.

Keba walked over and put a condom in my hand before pushing me in. "Second stall," she said.

I walked to the second stall and this girl named Carla was bent over with her pants down. She was almost nineteen years old, and still in the eleventh grade. She was medium height and thicker than a Snicker. She looked just like Fantasia, with her big ass and little waist. I slid my finger in her pussy from the back, and her pussy immediately grabbed my finger. Still feeling a little high from earlier, I was horny as fuck, and my dick stood straight out. I put the condom on, grabbed the base of my dick, and rubbed my dick head around the outer part of her pussy. She kept trying to push back on it, but I wouldn't let her. I kept teasing her until she screamed that she was cumming. I pushed all the way into her pussy.

Cum shot out of her pussy onto the toilet lid. It made me want to fuck her harder. I started pulling all the way out and then pushing back into her pussy.

"O … o … o … Ah!" she moaned.

I felt myself beginning to cum. I pulled out of her pussy, pulled the condom off, and came all over her ass.

Keba was licking her fingers and staring at me when I walked out of the stall. Her skirt was up around her waist. She walked to the stall where Carla was about to stand up. Keba pushed Carla back over the toilet, licked my cum off her ass, then started eating her from the back.

I tried to rush out of the bathroom, but I walked right into my teacher. She stood there staring at me with a red face. Her eyes moved down to my dick print. She licked her lips then took my ass to the principal's office. I had never been in any trouble before, so he let me off with a warning, but I had to pick up trash around the school.

At lunch, everyone called me the trashman. I left school with ten phone numbers, thanks to Tracy and Keba.

On our way home from school, Keba stopped and stared at me.

"Girl, what's wrong with you?" I asked.

"Promise me that regardless of how much pussy and money you get, you won't leave me."

"I promise. Can you do the same?"

"I can do more than promise. When we get to the house, ride with me."

I got in the car with Keba. Her car made my car look like a hooptie. I had no idea where we were going, but I trusted Keba, so I just enjoyed the ride. A few minutes later, we pulled up in front of the tattoo parlor.

"Why are we here?" I asked.

"Come on," she said, getting out of the car.

I followed her inside.

Keba went to the desk and I took a seat and flipped through the *Hip Hop Weekly* Magazine. She went behind a curtain and didn't come out until an hour later. Keba looked at me and smiled, so I got up and followed her to the car. She sat down in the driver's seat like her ass was hurting.

"What did you get?"

Keba pulled her shirt down and showed me a tattoo on her breast that had my name going through some pussy lips. She then turned to the side and lifted her skirt up. My name was displayed again, this time on a naked woman standing in water. She appeared to hold a sign with my name in cursive letters.

I reached over and tongued her with all I had.

"Anything else I gotta do to prove my love to you?"

"You didn't have to prove it then. I believed you."

I called my house on my cell and my mama picked up the phone.

"Boy, where the hell you at? Your daddy has been waiting for you! He is pissed the fuck off!"

"Damn ... tell—"

"Watch your damned mouth!" she said, cutting me off.

"Tell him I'm on my way," I said and hung up.

I leaned the seat back and thought about how I was gonna get at that nigga, Nitti. I know his bitch ass didn't make the call to kill Case if he's just a lieutenant.

We pulled up to Keba's yard and I kissed her on the lips. "I've got three of them that's responsible for your mother. I'm working on the other one now," I whispered in her ear.

She looked at me wide-eyed and kissed me again. This time, sucking on my bottom lip.

"I gotta go," I said, pushing her hand off my dick.

Ms. Towns came to the door with a package in her hand as I got out the car. I rushed home to where my dad was sitting on the porch.

"Let me tell your ass something. If you're not gonna be on time, don't waste my fucking time!" Johnny said with anger.

"Who the fuck—"

Before I could get it all out, Johnny had me in the collar against the house.

"Nigga, I don't care how much work you put in, or about this bullshit heroin. You will not disrespect me. Do you understand, nigga?" he said with spit flying in my face.

"I got you!"

I snatched away, wanting to go for my gun. This was my pops, so I went in the house.

Thirty minutes later, Johnny knocked on my door and walked in. I was lying on my bed, shining up my guns.

"The lawyer just called. He said he'll still see us today. We don't deal in emotions, we deal with them. I'll be waiting in the car," he said and walked out.

I put my guns up, grabbed my backpack, and filled the bag with money, except for about $10,000. I went to the car and got in. My mama came to the door and smiled at us leaving together.

We made it to The Mike Hill Law Firm in Rocky Mount a short time later. Mike Hill was a small white man with green eyes and black hair. His suit spelled money. As he shook both of our hands, he said to my pops, "Johnny, what brings you to see me? The last time I saw you, you wouldn't listen to me and the feds froze all of your accounts."

"Don't rub it in. My son wants to do a little investing with his bread and cover it up. We'll bring more money in the near future. I want him to see the business side of things."

"How much he got?" Mike asked like we were wasting his time.

"I got three hundred and eighty thousand," I said.

Both of them looked at me in shock.

"So what will you charge me?" I asked.

Mike grabbed his calculator and started hitting buttons. "I'll charge you $35,000."

"That's like, ten percent. That's too much. Let's go, Johnny." I got up to leave.

"Wait, little guy," Mike said, stopping me. "Give me twenty-five thousand, and you got yourself a deal."

"I'll do this, but if you shit on me, I'll kill you!" I reached in my pants and placed my gun on Mike's desk, then my money.

Mike's greedy ass grabbed the money and didn't pay the gun any mind.

"The paperwork will be ready tomorrow," he said as he counted the money.

As Johnny and I walked out of the office, Johnny turned back and stuck his head in Mike's office door.

"He's ahead of his time," Johnny said, causing Mike to smile.

On the way home, Johnny handed me a slip of paper. Nitti's name was at the top. His girlfriend's name and address were under it. I got a special treat for this nigga. *Damn, Case.*

I got in my car and called Tracy. She could easily pass for eighteen or nineteen years old. I got her to tell her mother that she was going to a friend's house. Y'all know she did it. I wrote down all the things that I needed before I picked Tracy up around the corner from her house. She must have thought I was gonna hit that because she wore a short skirt. We headed to a sex shop called Tape City in Rocky Mount. On the way there, I stopped by a hunting shop that sold knives, guns, clothes, and all type of hunting shit. I bought a big ass Rambo knife. Tracy kept rushing me so I couldn't look around like I really wanted to.

We finally made it to the sex shop and I sat in the car while she got the stuff I wanted. Her ass came out with two big bags and a small bag. I only wanted six items. Damn, she is pretty. She walks just like a model.

"You gonna give me some before I go home?" Tracy asked.

She turned to face me, put her back against the door, and pulled her skirt up. Not wearing any panties, Tracy spread her pussy lips and played with her clit. I opened the bag. It was filled with all kinds of sex toys, some of everything.

I pulled out an eight-inch vibrator, opened it, turned it on, and slid it in her pussy. Tracy almost jumped through the rolled up window. I fucked her with it all the way home. Halfway there, she pulled it out and turned her ass facing me. I fucked her from the back with it. Tracy had her face pressed against the window screaming. She was coming again when I pulled up around the corner from her house. I pulled the dildo out, and she flopped down on her seat breathing hard.

Tracy went into the bag and split the toys. She held up the dildo I had just used and licked all of her cum off it.

"I'll practice sucking with this one for you," Tracy said. "Give Keba her half."

"How do she know that we were together?" I asked.

"I told her where we were going."

"Get out of my car, snitch!"

Tracy burst out laughing and got out. She left a big ass wet spot in my seat. I drove home thinking about her crazy ass. When I pulled up, Keba was on her porch. I know she was waiting for me. She walked over to my car and got her bag out of the seat.

"Why didn't you ask me to ride with y'all?" Keba asked.

"Don't even start that shit!"

"No, I'm not tripping, I know you do shit for a reason. I was sitting at home bored out of my mind. We supposed to get our drivers licenses tomorrow, don't forget."

Keba kissed me on the lips then walked off with her toys. There ain't no telling what her freaky ass was going to do.

Johnny's car was gone. I already knew where he was. Pops was stacking that paper.

I started my car and drove to the other side of town. It was time to find this nigga, Nitti. I rode by his girlfriend's house and parked down the street. With my hood up, I watched the house until dark. Once night fell, I put the hood down and sat in the car. Not even knowing how the nigga looked, I picked up the phone and called Keba.

"Hellooo," Keba moaned.

"Stop for a minute, bae." I could hear the vibrator buzzing then it was turned off.

"What, bae?"

"I need you to find out what that nigga, Nitti, looks like. The one that be on the west side."

"Alright, I'll call you back."

A black 2004 Acura pulled up in Nitti's girlfriend's yard. A light-skinned girl got out of the car. She was about twenty-five years old and she was an amazon, standing at about 5'9" and every bit of two hundred pounds. A brown-skinned little boy about eight years old got out of the back seat. I waited for two more hours then decided to go home. My phone rang as I pulled off, then beeped with a message.

"Hello," I answered.

"Did you get the pictures?" Keba asked.

"Yeah, I haven't checked them yet."

"It's one of Nitti and one of me."

"How did you get the picture?"

"He was fucking my friend Veda's, aunt on the west side. She had a picture of him."

"I'm on my way home. I'm tired."

"You coming over tonight?"

"No, I'll see you in the morning."

"Alright, I love you." She hung up.

I pulled into the driveway and noticed that Johnny still wasn't home. After I went in the house and fixed a bowl of Fruit Loops, I fell asleep on the couch. Johnny opening the door woke me up. He walked in with a tote bag.

"Don't forget we're supposed to sign the papers tomorrow, and you got to go get your driver's license," Johnny said, pulling stacks of money out the bag.

"You sold the whole brick already?" I asked, looking at the money.

"No, this is what we've made in the last couple of days."

"How much is it?"

"Seventy-five thousand, and I still got the fifty thousand in the stash."

"You doing your thing, ain't you, Dad?"

"Let's just hope this shit goes as planned. We don't buy no flashy shit until we retire. We don't need the heat," Johnny said as he stretched. "I'll see you tomorrow."

He handed me the bag and walked to his room. I was not about to keep extra money in the house. I went over to Arkeba's. This time, there were no bricks under her window. I dialed her number as I looked through the window. She lay asleep on the bed, naked.

"Hello," she answered sleepily.

"Keba ... help ... me!" I whispered, trying not to laugh.

"What? Where are you?" Keba almost yelled. She put on her shoes, tripped over her clothes and fell to the floor.

I tried not to laugh, but it came out. I knocked on the window.

Keba ran to the window, pulled it up, then walked away. I stepped through the window with the bag on my arm. She turned around with tears rolling down her cheeks. I felt bad after that.

"What's wrong, bae? I was just playing."

"Don't scare me like that. I thought something had happened to you!" she cried.

I held out my arms.

She walked to me and hugged me tight.

"What's the bag for?" she asked, wiping her eyes.

"It's some money. Put this up 'til tomorrow."

Keba didn't even open the bag. She just put it in her closet. I undressed down to my boxers and got in bed. Keba got in bed with me and laid her head on my chest.

We woke up to her alarm going off the next morning. I jumped up, scared to death, looking for Ms. Towns. I got the bag out of the closet, put my clothes on, went back out the window, and ran home. After sneaking back into my room, I checked the pictures Keba had sent me on my phone. One was of Nitti. He was dark skinned, late twenties, short and slim built. He had lines cut into his hair like waves. I went to the next picture, and Keba was lying on her bed naked, with all her sex toys between her legs.

I smiled then got in the shower for school.

Chapter 8

Man

Three Months Later

"Brown, you have a visit!" the fat white janitor yelled. I have started talking to my damn self. This shit will make you do shit you never thought you would do. Who the fuck here to see me this early?

The female jailer stood in the visiting area. She looked at me and licked her lips. This shit done fucked me up! She probably wasn't even looking at me. She was about 30 years old, medium height, with a slender build, but thick in the thighs and ass, brown-skinned, with micro braids.

I walked into the booth and saw Nitti. *Why the fuck is he here?* I wondered. The damn feds or anybody could be watching. I picked up the phone and stared at him. This shit gotta be serious.

"What's good, my nigga?" I asked.

"Shit, big bruh, just holding it down," Nitti said.

"What brings you here?"

"Our money is straight, but your boy back on, and he's flooding two towns with the best boy that's been around in a long time."

"Is that right? Put that nigga to sleep. Start with his mama."

"You're still the boss. I'm on it." Nitti put his fist to the glass and I gave it back. "Oh, tell that jailer bitch I'll meet her at Popeye's at nine o'clock. Tell her scared money don't make no money."

I smiled at him. Bruh, you know I go to court Monday, right?"

"Yeah, I know. I'm going to give you a going away gift."

I had to shake my head at my lieutenant. He was trained to go. Nitti had been running my business since I've been gone. Now, this bitch ass Johnny wants to be in the way. I'm not going for that shit.

When I walked out of the visiting booth, the woman jailer was still there. Instead of telling her what Nitti said, I blew a kiss at her. She knew who the fuck I was if she knew Nitti. The bitch turned her back on me and called the jailer to come get me. Fuck her. When I get to prison, I'm gonna buy me some damn pussy. She don't think that I'm broke, do she? A fifteen-year heroin run, y'all do the math.

The fat white jailer told me to come along as he walked, sounding out of breath. I made it back to the cellblock and saw that they had put a wino in there. His feet smelled like rotten shit. His ass has to go, fuck that!

Nitti

I know y'all are wondering why I am gonna fuck with that man's mama. If y'all don't like it, y'all can get it too! Man took care of me since I was a youngin. If it wasn't for him, I don't know where I would be. My money is super straight. I drive a gray Bentley GT, and I live in a condo. All because of Man. I got to ride for my nigga. Y'all don't know what it's like to grow up with both of your parents on heroin and to watch them both die of AIDS. Man showed me how to be a man, so I gotta show that love and loyalty back, by any means necessary.

I decided to stop by my baby mom's crib first. She has been tripping about me not being around. Oh, shit! I drive too fast. I almost ran over this black skinny ass little girl jumping rope in front of Ashley's house. The little bitch was fast, though. I can't stop laughing. This bitch ain't even home. I backed straight back out and headed to our stash spot down from Johnny's mother's crib. I'll chill there and play the game until it gets dark. My lying ass baby mama said she was home. I knew her hoe ass was lying because I heard niggas in the background. She knows not to have niggas in shit I pay for.

I pulled up at the stash spot, and the old lady next door waved at me. If I didn't get her grass cut when we cut ours, she probably wouldn't even speak. Everybody fake these days. It's all about what they can get out of you.

Two hours later, I peeked out the window. It had turned jet black outside. I went and changed into all black. After creeping out the back door, I ran through the back yard until I reached Johnny's mother's back door. I knocked on her door like I was the police.

"Who the hell at my damn back door?" she yelled.

"Ms. Bullock, it's me, Nitti, Johnny's friend. He's been shot. He told me to bring him here!" I said in a scared tone.

Mrs. Bullock looked out of her window. She didn't know my face, but I knew she would open the door to see what was going on. From what I'd heard, she didn't play when it came to her only son. Mrs. Bullock snatched the door open, and I punched her in the mouth with all I had. She fell back on the kitchen table in a daze. I hit her again, knocking her out cold.

"Damn, bitch, you took two of these!" I said to her unconscious body, holding up my two fists.

I dragged her to the first room I got to, ripped off her clothes, and tied her down on her stomach. She woke up naked and gagged. I sat on the bed next to her, eating a piece of her strawberry cake.

"This is good, real good," I said, finishing my last piece.

She tried to talk to me, but I wasn't trying to hear shit she had to say. I reached back and pushed my finger in her pussy. Damn, that shit was tight and warm. Fuck y'all! Pussy is pussy. I pulled my pants and boxers to my ankles, put on a condom, and went in that pussy from the back. She turned her ass back and forth like I was killing her. They call me last long time Nitti. I fucked her for about twenty minutes. Y'all think I'm lying; the old bitch nutted about three times. I always wondered if a bitch getting raped could cum. Now I know.

The pussy was so good, I had to try the ass out. I spread her fat cheeks and rammed my dick in her ass. She screamed through the gag, but that didn't help. I was in my zone. I'm glad I wore a rubber, because when I pulled out, I had shit and blood all over my dick. I stuck it right back in her pussy, and I came again.

She lay there crying. No sympathy for the enemy, that's what Man taught me. I walked through the house and found some bananas on the kitchen table. I grabbed three of them and walked back into the room laughing. I pushed one huge banana in her pussy and one in her ass until the stem disappeared. I took the gag out of her mouth, pulled her mouth open, and pushed the other banana down her throat. She tried to bite it to keep from choking, but I held her mouth open and pushed. Her eyes bulged out and she soon lost consciousness. Holding her head back, I pulled out my razor and cut her throat. Blood gushed out onto the sheets.

I went to the bathroom, flushed the razor and condom, washed my hands, and walked to the back door. I turned back and took the whole cake plate. That strawberry cake was off the chain. There was no need to close the back door. I wrote, *scared money don't make no money*, on the screen door with cake icing and walked off.

Now y'all tell me I ain't the truth. Y'all probably feel some type of way about what I've done. If the boss sends me to see y'all, I'm coming, so play your fucking position.

I went back to the stash spot, showered, and put my same clothes back on that I wore to the stash spot. Twenty minutes later, I walked out the front door with my cake in my hand. I put it on the passenger seat and drove off. At the Arab store, I called the police and told them a white male was seen running out of the house next door. Shit, them crackers do it to us.

"Johnny where are you?" I sang as I got back into my car.

Jason

That motherfucker almost ran me over. Yeah, that was me who was dressed up like a girl, jumping rope. I have been laying on this nigga Nitti. He's been missing in action. I tried to jump up and shoot at his ass, but my damn gun flew the other way and I couldn't get to it. By the time I ran around the corner to my car, that nigga was long gone. I had been sitting on this nigga for three months, and I lost him like that! I'm going the fuck home.

I waited a couple of hours then drove off. When I pulled up in my driveway, everybody was gone. I checked my phone before I got out the car and saw that I had about twenty missed calls, all from Keba and my mama. I checked my texts and one read, *Your grandmama!!!*

I jumped back in my car and did everything on my dash to grandma's house. Two cops had blue lighted me, but I wasn't stopping until I got there. When I pulled up and got out, the police were everywhere. They all surrounded me.

My mother ran through the crowd, screaming, "No … no … that's my baby!"

"Get on the ground!" they kept yelling.

I got on the ground.

They ran over and tried to put cuffs on me.

"Grandma! Grandma!" I screamed over and over.

After placing me in the police car, they questioned my mother. The other cops told them what had happened. The officers felt sympathy for me and let me go, after giving me two tickets. One of the cops took the cuffs off. I ran to the yellow tape. A black cop pushed me back. He looked just like the black cop with the afro from *Boys in the Hood*, except he had a bald head. I saw my dad on his knees crying, so I ran to where he was and grabbed his arms.

"Get up, Da, get up!" I pulled him up, but he flopped back down.

"They killed my mama, Jay! They killed my mama!" he cried.

After a few minutes passed, my mama and I were finally able to pick Johnny up. We held him up all the way to the car. My mama let him go to open my car door. He snatched away and ran back to the yellow tape. After tearing the tape down, he kept running. It took four police to bring him down. While he was on the ground, the rescue workers brought Grandma out in a body bag.

"Mama … mama … mama!" Johnny screamed until he ran out of breath.

The same two white detectives who showed up at Ms. Towns' house, came out of the house. After they watched the rescue workers pull off, they told the cops to let Johnny up. Johnny got up, looking for the ambulance, but it had already left.

"Mr. Bullock … can we ask you a few questions?" Detective Smith asked. Johnny just stood there in a daze. "Are you familiar with the phrase, 'scared money don't make no money'?"

Johnny looked at the detectives like he knew something, then shook his head no.

"Whoever did this meant to send a message, so it had to have been someone that you or your mother knew."

"What did they do to my mother?" Johnny asked.

"I'd rather not …"

"What did they do to my mother?" Johnny yelled, cutting the detective off.

"They raped her, forced bananas into her vagina, rectum, and down her throat. Then they cut her throat."

I walked off, madder than I think I've ever been, but I didn't know where to start. After the last police left, Johnny, my mama, and I entered the house. There was not a thing out of place in the front room. We followed Johnny to the first guest room. He opened the door and started crying. Grandma's blood had soaked through the covers and sheets that the police took, and onto the mattress. Johnny rubbed the bloody spot. He looked down at the cake crumbs on the floor and kept rubbing the bloody spot.

I cried silently for my grandmother, and for my father's hurt. He always seemed to be so strong. I kneeled beside him and pulled him to me.

"Who did this, Pops?" I whispered.

He seemed to be in a daze. Johnny staggered to his room and came back out with a half-gallon of gin. My mother watched us walk to my grandmama's kitchen table, and walked off to give us some privacy. Johnny got up, went to the cabinet, and brought back two glasses. He poured a shot for me and one for himself. I had never drank liquor in my life. Johnny turned his up, so I turned mine up. That shit liked to killed me, but I had to show Pops that I was with him. He poured us both another cup. I let mine sit, he dumped his down and poured another cup.

"When I was a little guy, about ten years old, this guy named Man moved into our neighborhood. We became friends fast after we had a good fight against each other. One day, we found his mama's stash of weed. It was about two ounces. Man wanted to smoke it up, and I wanted to sell it. He was scared to go to the other hood next door to ours and hustle. So, I always said, 'scared money don't make no money.' We even lost our virginity together. And he had somebody kill my mama!" Johnny threw his glass, shattering it against the wall.

My mama rushed back into the room. She picked up the broom and swept the glass up without saying a word.

"That nigga ate at my mama's table!" Johnny yelled. "He set me up with the feds, and I still let his ass live. Then he still do some fuck shit? It's on now!"

"Where he at?"

"He's in jail for killing his bitch, but we're going to pay his aunt a visit. Then we're going to kill every nigga that has any ties with him. Come with me!"

He led me outside to Grandma's barn. Johnny did something to the light switch and the damn wall slid back. Nothing but guns showed. He started pulling down AK-47s, M16s, Mac 11s, and .45s. He even had silencers to the .45s.

We went back to the house. Johnny almost tripped, causing him to look down. Cake crumbs were on the doorstep. He ran into the house and looked at the counter.

"Whoever killed my mama ate her cake or took it with them!"

The glass on the back door had been taken as evidence. Johnny sat back down at the kitchen table and drank out of the cup that he had poured me. He got up from the table, went to his room, and came back wearing all black. Johnny walked out of the house without saying a word. I grabbed two 45s and followed him to my car.

"Be careful!" my mama yelled.

Johnny got in the driver seat, and I hopped in on the passenger side. He drove until we got on the outskirts of Tarboro. A long paved driveway soon showed to the left. Johnny turned down the paved road. It led to a big house. I looked over at Pops and wondered what he was thinking.

Johnny

Niggas gonna die! I'm killing them all! That's the only phrase that keeps playing in my head. That bitch ass nigga, Man, had my mom killed! He doesn't know that I used to fuck his aunt before I went to prison. Soon as I got home, she called my mama and gave her the address and phone number to give to me. The whole time I was locked up, I didn't get a letter, a picture, or a money order from her. The sad part about it is, she don't know that I saw her name on a statement she wrote about me to the feds. Man got her in the cut, so niggas can't get to her, but shit is about to get real.

"Get down, Jason," I said when we pulled into the driveway.

Jason squatted down in his seat.

"When I get in the house, in about three to five minutes, or when you hear moaning, search everything," I said.

Renee came to the door in a sheer white robe. I got out of the car, walked up the steps and unfastened her robe. She stood there naked, looking like a forty-five-year-old Kelly Rowland. Renee stepped back into the house, unfastening my pants. She snatched my pants and boxers down and I stepped out of them, leaving them at the front door. Renee then pulled my shirt over my head. She stepped back and looked at my muscled body, grabbed my dick, and pulled me behind her up the stairs to the first room.

She had different flavored condoms on the nightstand. I cracked a smile. Here she was holding my dick, and we still hadn't said a word to each other. We never talked until we started fucking. She grabbed an orange condom, walked up to me, got on her knees, and licked me from my inner thigh to my balls. Renee lifted my balls up and licked under them. My dick stood straight out.

I pulled her up by her hair, turned her around and pushed her over the bed. She tried to stand up, but I held her in place until I put my condom on. I pushed four inches into her pussy.

"Ah … wait … Ah …wait!" She let out a sound that was part moan and part scream.

Renee reached back and spread her ass cheeks while looking back at me. She had an 'it hurts' expression on her face. I pushed six more inches into her pussy.

"Why … you ah … oh … didn't … write … oh … meee!" She moaned.

I slid my thumb into her ass. Renee moved in circles on my

dick and hand. I pulled my thumb out her ass, and she reached back and put her middle finger in there. I started pounding her pussy with all twelve inches.

"What ... oh ... I ... ooh ... oh ... do? What ... I ... oh ... oh ... do?" She took her finger out of her ass and started throwing it back on my dick.

"I'm cumin.' Oh ... oh ... stay ... oh ... the ... night!" she said as she came.

Renee tried to slide up so my dick would come out of her pussy. I turned her around, slid her on the bed, put my dick all the way in her pussy, pushed her legs back and went dick diving.

My dick came out, and Renee opened her pussy lips for me to enter. She then put her hand on my chest so I couldn't put it all in. I pushed her hands away and went all the way in her.

"Sto ... o ... o ...! I ... miss ... oh ... u!"

Jason

"Enough ... enou ... e ... e ... oh!" she moaned.

Damn, Pops killing that pussy! I thought as I crept back down the stairs. I had checked every room. What the fuck did Pop want me to look for? He didn't even say. I think Pops just wanted some new pussy to relieve some stress. I moved into the kitchen where a strawberry cake sat on the counter. It made me think about Grandma. I grabbed a knife and cut a piece. If I have to wait for Pops, I might as well eat. I went to the refrigerator and got some milk then sat down on the stool.

I bit the cake and looked at it. I took another bite. Maybe it's just my taste buds. I gotta let Johnny taste this. I cut him a small piece, put it on a paper plate, and walked up the stairs. When I got to the room, I chuckled. Johnny had the lady's legs pushed back to her ears. She was moaning and groaning, asking him to stop, but still meeting every stroke.

"Johnny, you need to taste this!" I said, causing her to jump.

Johnny pulled out of her pussy when he heard my voice. She rolled away from him then looked at the door.

"Who the fuck are you?" she asked weakly.

Johnny walked to me butt naked and took the cake. His eyes bulged when he bit into it.

"I don't know who the fuck—"

"Bitch, where the fuck you get this cake from?" Johnny asked, cutting her off.

"No, motherfucker, who the fuck is this?" she said, pointing her short, manicured nail at me.

I handed Johnny the .45.

"Bitch, you better tell me where you got this cake from!" Johnny yelled.

"One of Man's friends dropped by. He was eating some, and he gave me the rest."

"Friend who?"

"Why?"

Boom! Johnny shot her in the arm.

Johnny

This bitch think I'm playing with her! I went across the hallway, took the condom off, flushed it, then ran downstairs to get my clothes. I checked the doors and saw an ax next to the kitchen door.

"Jay, bring her down here!" I yelled.

Jason dragged her down the stairs into the kitchen.

"Get the fuck off of me," Renee screamed. "Help … help!"

"Shut up, bitch!" Jason yelled. He grabbed the broomstick and shoved it in her pussy until it broke off.

"Bitch, where you get that cake from?" I asked. She lay there in pain. "Jay, stretch this bitch's good arm out," I said to Jason.

He grabbed her arm and stretched it out. I took one hard swing.

Her arm shot off and hit the stove. Blood sprayed all over Jason's face.

"Bitch, what the fuck is his name?" I asked.

"Nitti!" she yelled.

Jason and I looked at each other. Jason snatched the ax out of my hand, grabbed Renee's injured arm, spread it out, and chopped it off. The floor was painted with blood.

"Money ... I have! Have ... money!" Renee said with blood running out the side of her mouth.

"Where?" Jason asked.

"Pull ... rug ... under ... sink ... I ... cold!"

Jason dropped the ax and ran to the bathroom. I pulled Renee's legs apart as she coughed up blood. I drew the ax high and came down, cutting deep into her thigh. I drew back again and connected. Her leg slid off in the blood. Again, I raised the ax and cut off her other leg in one strike.

"Now you look like a rat, bitch!" I said as blood dripped off my face.

Jason came in the room with two pillowcases filled with money, and one that was half-full. All I remember after that is the cold water coming out of the shower. That shit was cold too! Jason stood there watching me as I grabbed the soap and washed all the blood off of me. Then I rinsed off and got out of the shower. I dried off with a towel, cleaned the tub with Clorox, and made sure that I poured some down the drain. I put on the clothes that Jason had found for me in a closet. Finally, I put the soap, towel, condom, wrapper and the clothes that I wore there in a trash bag and left the bathroom.

Jason had used a mop to clean up our footprints by the time I walked into the front room. I dialed 911 on Renee's house phone, grabbed my mama's cake and the trash bag, then walked out of the house. Jason followed with the money.

"Where to now?" Jason asked, pulling out of the driveway.

"Let's pay his block pushers a visit," I said, holding my mama's cake.

Jason and I pulled up in front of my mama's house. I got out and ran to the barn. Three minutes later, I returned to the car with an AK and two Mac 11s. As Jason pulled off, I spotted Jean looking out the window at us. I gave Jason the address. A few minutes later, we parked down the street and walked to them nigga's spot. They had music playing. I looked through the window and saw two niggas playing the game while the other two watched.

"Jay, come here!" I whispered. Jason crept over to me. "When I kick the door in and start shooting, you back me in case I miss someone. If you look in there and everyone is laid down, run to the car and start it up.!"

"I gotcha!" Jason whispered.

I kicked the door open and shot two of them down. The other two tried to run to the table and get their guns, but I opened their backs up with the AK. I walked over to each of them and gave them headshots. "Fuck niggas," I mumbled as I ran out of the house and down the street.

Jason saw me coming and drove to meet me.

I hopped in the back seat and he pulled off slowly.

"Drive across town to the south side," I said.

"The police gonna set up a road block sooner or later," Jason advised me.

"We'll drive all the way around to get home."

Jason drove past about seven guys standing in front of an apartment building.

I handed him one of my Mac 11s. "Let's make it do what it do," I said.

We parked down the street. It was easy to creep up on the niggas. They were making heroin sales, passing a blunt of weed around. We hit corners on them, with the guns already pointed. When they saw the guns, they tried to run. Jason and I shot their asses down! We stood over them and finished them off. Straight head shots.

Jason and I ran back to the car and drove off in the opposite direction. I looked in the back seat and almost shit my pants. I had forgotten about the black trash bags and pillowcases of money. I gotta focus! I'm slipping. They took my mama though, y'all.

Jason and I pulled up at my mama's house. I stashed the guns back behind the wall and set the bloody clothes on fire in a trash barrel. Jason took the pillowcases of money in the house.

Jean ran outside and hugged Jason. I walked past her to the car and got my mama's cake. In the kitchen, I set it back in the cake dish on her counter.

Chapter 9

Man

TARBORO'S DEADLIEST NIGHT OF ALL TIME! What the fuck! I snatched the newspaper out of the young guy's hand. On the front of the paper were photos of the thirteen people who had been killed. When my eyes landed on the photo of my auntie, I lost it. I punched every person that I got my hands on before the guards came and tasered my ass.

A few hours later, I woke up in the hole with the newspaper on the cell bars. I picked the paper up and started to read. First, the article talked about what happened to Johnny's mother. I couldn't help but to smile. The piece went on to mention the eleven guys who were shot and killed in my spots, and finally the details of my auntie's murder were provided. My only living blood on my mama side! She was raped with a broomstick and had her limbs cut off.

I tried to hold it in, but it came out loud. I heard a guy down the hallway say, "Listen to this bitch ass nigga crying!"

My mama and bitch ass daddy died years ago. Auntie took me in at fifteen years old and raised me. Niggas gonna pay for this! They killed my workers. Fuck them, they can be replaced. Nitti should've killed Johnny right after that. I forgot to tell him how ruthless Johnny used to be. I know they got my money out of her house. Damn, Auntie, I'm so sorry! I can't even go to her funeral. I began to cry again, but I quickly wiped my eyes and started doing push-ups.

"Brown, you got a visit," the fat jailer said.

I stepped in the orange jumpsuit and yelled that I was ready. They had to shackle me because I had blanked out earlier. I took baby steps to the visiting booth, with the shackles and handcuffs on. I kept picturing my auntie lying on the floor with her legs and arms missing and a broken broomstick in her pussy.

Nitti sat on the other side of the glass smiling as I entered the visiting booth.

"You should be smiling. First mission accomplished," Nitti said.

"What the fuck is there to smile about? Have you seen this?" I yelled, putting the clip to the window.

Nitti's smile turned to a frown, then tears rushed out of his eyes. All of his boys were killed, and Auntie was like a mama to him also. He wiped his tears away.

"Who did this?" Nitti asked.

"You already know where the hit came from."

"How did he know where she lived?"

"I don't know, but I want him gone by the time I go to court tomorrow. And do his ass real dirty."

"Say no more!"

"Alright, be safe out there."

"Don't worry about me, I'm good."

I put my fist to the window and Nitti did the same. Tears danced in the corner of my eyes as I walked out the booth. I gotta get out of this jail before I go crazy! The same woman jailer stood there talking to another woman jailer about what happened last night.

"Ms. Bullock was a sweet lady. We went to the same church, and she could cook the best strawberry cakes," she said.

I walked up to her like I was gonna ask her something, and

head butted that bitch in her mouth. Two of her teeth broke off in my forehead. She fell to the floor holding her mouth, as I stood over her with blood dripping from my forehead. The guards maced me. I was blind, then they beat the living shit out of me. No lie, I actually shit on myself. After they finished beating me, they dragged me back to the hole and threw me back into the cell.

On the cold floor, I lay laughing at that bitch still screaming about her teeth. The mace on my face began to feel hotter and hotter. I hopped up, ran to the sink, and rinsed most of the mace off of me. Looking in the mirror, I saw two of the bitch's broken teeth sticking out of my forehead. I reached up and pulled them out. As blood dripped into the sink, I burst out laughing again. I couldn't stop laughing this time as I lay down on my bunk with shit still in my drawers.

I woke up later in a cold sweat. Something ain't right.

Nitti

I'm second guessing myself about killing that man's mama now. I didn't know that nigga go that hard. I would have fallen the fuck back and killed them together. Where can I find this nigga? I have been riding around asking about him all day. This nigga hiding. I gotta go check on Ashley and my son, Dime. They are all I have left in this world besides Man, and he's about to leave me. Maybe a little bit of Ashley's pussy will ease the stress,

I turned into the driveway and parked behind Ashley's car. Leaning over, I reached into my glove compartment and pulled out my .38 special. I didn't want to give her crazy ass no gun, but too much shit is going on. After I let myself into the house, I went to check on Dime first. He favored my pops a lot. Dime has long cornrows that he hates to get braided. He slept in his bed, holding a cap gun that I thought was real when I first entered the room. I had to smile to myself, because of what I had created.

I tiptoed to Ashley's room. She lay on the bed naked, with a small fan blowing on her bald pussy. To be on the big side, she had some small pussy lips. My dick instantly got hard. After undressing, I walked to the head of the bed and rubbed my dick all over her face and lips.

"Damn, what a way to wake up," Ashley said when she opened her eyes.

She grabbed my dick and sucked on the head. Her mouth felt like a suction cup. That's why I can't leave this bitch alone. She sucks dick so good! Her mouth stay warm and wet. Ashley turned to the side so I could fuck her mouth like I wanted to. I didn't want to cum, so I went all the way down her throat and back out real slow. Every time I would go in and get ready to pull out, she would wrap her lips around my dick and open them when I pushed back in. Ashley fingered her pussy at the same time. I had to pull out before I came.

She got on all fours, reached under, and spread her pussy lips open. I pushed in her pussy from the back. She moaned loud, letting her pussy muscles grip and release my dick. I spread her ass cheeks apart and watched my dick go in and out. Her wetness made my dick shine. Y'all can say what y'all want. Them big girls got the best pussy. I pulled out of her pussy except the head. She moved in circles on the head of my dick. I stood on my tip toes, feeling the inside of her pussy grind against my dick. Ashley's thick white cum sat on the tip of my dick. She turned around and licked it off.

Fuck that! I got to taste this pussy. I started sucking one nipple and squeezing the other one. She yelled that she was about to cum. Damn I love this hoe. I licked down to her pussy lips. Ashley's pussy was super wet. I opened her pussy lips, making her clit slide out slowly. I sucked on the tip of it, just like she did my dick head. She moaned loud and curled her toes. I moved up and down on her clit as Ashley pulled on the sheets. Her whole body trembled as she came again. I let her clit go and tickled the tip of it with my tongue.

Ashley tried to close her legs and slide away, but I held them open and kept tickling her clit. Cum ran out of her pussy like running water. I gladly licked it all up. She was out of it and didn't want any more. I knew that her clit had become sensitive. I pushed my dick deep in her pussy missionary style and put them big red legs on my shoulders as I pounded her pussy. To keep her from moaning too loud, I put two fingers in her mouth. She sucked on them like they were my dick. Ashley's pussy got wetter and tighter the more we fucked. I went harder and faster in her pussy. She sucked harder on my fingers as I came deep in her pussy and dropped down on top of her. This bitch got me gone.

I lay on her for a minute then rolled off. Ashley got up, went to the bathroom, came back and washed me off. My cum ran out of her pussy. She wiped it with her hand and licked it off. Y'all talking about pussy can't put a nigga to sleep. I rolled over and was snoring two minutes later.

When I woke up, it was just about to be dark. I heard Ashley yell for Dime to come in the house. We call him Dime because this little nigga used to always ask people for a dime when he was about two years old. He was smart. He knew they weren't going to just give him a dime, so the name stuck.

"Ma, my friend wants some water," Dime said.

"Tell her she can have some water, then she gotta go home. She's too big to be playing with you anyway."

I walked into the kitchen in my boxer shorts. The same little girl I almost ran over stood in the living room. She was ugly too. I turned my Kool-Aid up and started thinking about how she dove out of the way that day. I burst out laughing and red Kool-Aid flew all over the floor.

"Ma … Ma!" Dime yelled.

The girl had my son in a chokehold with a gun to his head. The glass slipped from my hand and shattered on the floor.

"Oh my God!" Ashley yelled.

"Wait … little girl … wait!" I said.

Jason

"Bitch nigga, ain't no little girl here!"

Nitti looked shocked that I was actually a boy. I got this nigga now. I kicked my bag to the middle of the floor.

"I want both of y'all to strip ass naked right now if y'all don't want me to blow his fucking head off.

Ashley and Nitti took their clothes off in a hurry as Dime cried.

"Please … please don't hurt him!" Ashley said, standing there naked.

"Look in that bag and put them cuffs on Nitti from the back," I said.

She tried to leave them loose, but I was up on game.

"Bitch, you better tighten them cuffs up!" I said.

Ashley jumped and squeezed the cuffs tight, causing Nitti to flinch.

"Alright, get those ties and put them around his legs."

She did as I said with shaky hands.

"I got money, lil nigga … shit don't have to be like this!" Nitti said.

"Walk backward to me," I told Ashley. She walked backward to me, visibly trembling. "Put your hands behind your back."

I pushed Dime to the floor and put the handcuffs on her. Dime stood there scared. He had peed all over himself. I put the gun on my waist and pulled my Rambo knife out of the holster. I bent down to put the ties on Ashley's legs. This bitch tried to kick me. I raised my knife and came down on her foot. I could feel the knife going through her bones.

Ashley yelled, causing Dime to run to her aid.

"Leave my momma alone!" Dime yelled with his fists balled up.

I pushed his little ass on the floor.

He balled up and cried.

"Chill, man ... chill!" Nitti yelled. "They're gonna do what you say!"

I snatched my knife back out of her foot. She screamed with all she had. I got something for their ass when I get these ties on this bitch's legs. I grabbed Dime and put ties on his hands and legs. I then pushed them over on the floor, turned them over and dragged them to a sitting up position in front of the couch.

I dialed Johnny's number on my cell phone.

"Hello," he answered in a sad tone.

"I got him," I said.

"Where the fuck are you at?"

"I'll handle him, just hold on until he tells me where the stash house at."

I laid the phone down.

"Just let us go. You can have all the money," Nitti said.

"You're gonna tell me anyway."

I walked up to Dime and put the bloody knife to his eye.

"Alright ... chill!" Nitti yelled. "The first house on the corner down from ... Johnny's mama house."

I got angry all over again when I heard that, and picked up my phone. "You hear that?" I asked Johnny.

"Yeah, I'm going right now, I'll hit you back," Johnny said and hung up.

"Why are you doing this?" Ashley asked.

"Before we play our little game, tell her what you did."

Ashley looked at Nitti, who sat there quiet as Dime cried loudly. I went in the bag and taped his mouth shut.

"I'll tell you what he did. He went to my grandmama's house ..." Nitti's eyes flew open. "Yes, my grandmama, and beat her in the face. He then tied her down naked, raped her in her pussy and ass, stuffed bananas in her holes, even her mouth, then cut her throat!"

Ashley threw up all over herself. She looked at Nitti, then headbutted him in the face, busting his lip.

"How could you put us in danger like this? You promised that we would always be safe!" she cried, still in pain.

I opened the front door. After observing the area, I went on the side of the house and came back with a bigger Tape City bag. I closed the door, locked it, went into the bag and pulled out some sex dice.

"Alright, this is a matter of life and death. Whatever the dice lands on, that's what you gotta do," I said, looking at Ashley. I rolled the dice and they landed on pussy and dick. "The first one that gets to three points wins. If I win, somebody dies. If you win, somebody lives."

Ashley thought I was talking about my dick. She was ready to win the first point.

"How am I gonna do it in these?" She held up the cuffs.

"Put your hands on the back of the chair and push up," I said.

I went into the bag and pulled out a twelve-inch dildo. It was the width of a soda can.

"I can't ... no ... I can't!" Ashley said, flopping back to the floor.

My phone rang.

"What's up?" I answered.

"Make that nigga tell you exactly where the money at!" Johnny said.

"Where the bread at?" I asked Nitti.

"Let my family go first," Nitti said with an attitude.

"Hold on, Johnny." I grabbed my knife and started sawing his little toe off. Blood shot out onto my neck.

"Oh shit!" he screamed. "In the back room closet. Push the wall back."

"I got it, Jay, punish his bitch ass like he did my mama!"

"I got you," I said and hung up.

"Now, where were we? The game plan changed. For every point I get, I get to cut off a toe, starting with Dime."

"Alright, I'll do it!" Ashley said.

She pushed up on the chair. I slid the toy up under her, placing the head at her pussy entrance. Ashley tried to slide down slow. She couldn't get but about two inches in. The rest wouldn't go. She screamed. Her arm slipped off of the couch, and she fell over in Nitti's lap. She saw me walking toward Dime. Little snot bubbles came out of his nose. Ashley reached back and tried to push more in, but it still wouldn't go.

"Time's up." I reached down and cut off Dime's pinky toe. He screamed and cried through the tape.

"Nooo ... nooo!" Ashley cried, laying in Nitti's lap.

"Come on, man!" Nitti said with tears running down his face.

"Alright, here's the second roll." One dice landed on suck, and the other one landed on ass. "Okay, you gotta suck dick and tongue their ass."

Ashley wiped her tears away. She knew that she could do that. Ashley leaned over further and tried to put Nitti's dick in her mouth.

"No, not his dick."

Ashley looked up at me with a question in her eyes.

I walked over to Dime and snatched his pissy pants and Batman drawers to his ankles. "I'm talking about his."

Ashley began to cry harder.

"Don't do it, baby! He gonna ..."

Before Nitti could finish, I stabbed him in the jaw with my knife. It came through on the other side of his face, cutting half his tongue off. I pulled my knife out of his jaw and he spit blood and half of his tongue out onto the floor.

"Next time you speak without being spoken to, I'll cut that little nigga's head off. Now, Ashley, where were we?"

I pulled her out of Nitti's lap and leaned her over into Dime's lap, so his little dick was right at her lips.

"Do I have to make another point?"

Ashley shook her head no and put Dime's dick in her mouth. She cried and moved her head up and down. I watched her suck him for five minutes then I flipped him over.

"You know what to do," I said.

Ashley slid her tongue into the crack of lil' Dime's ass and acted like she had pushed it in.

"Bitch, do you think I'm stupid?"

She pushed in and out with her tongue as tears dropped on his little butt. Nitti sat there crying, with blood running out of his mouth.

"Nigga, ain't no need to cry now. You wasn't crying when you did my grandmama dirty."

I stopped Ashley and pulled Dime's pants up.

"Can you please let me and my baby go now?" Ashley asked.

Before I could respond, Nitti spit blood all over my legs, then tried to say, fuck me. I stared at the nigga for a minute.

"So, you're willing to do anything to get you and your son out of this?" I asked Ashley.

"Yes!" she cried.

I turned her to the side, took off the cuffs, and dropped my knife in her lap. Pointing the gun at her, I said, "Pick up the knife!" She picked it up. "Since this bitch ass nigga got balls enough to spit on me, I want to kill that problem. Cut his fucking balls off."

Ashley hesitated. I put my gun to Dime's head. She pushed Nitti over, and he tried to kick her away. Ashley grabbed him by the balls and he yelled. She looked back at me holding the gun to Dime's head. Ashley lifted Nitti's dick and cut his balls out of the sack. They fell to the floor as blood ran everywhere. Ashley sat up and rocked back and forth in a daze. She had dropped the knife on the floor.

"Nitti … Nitti …!" I said.

He would not say anything until I grabbed the knife off the floor and snatched the tape off of his son's mouth.

"Ma … Da … Ma!" he cried.

Nitti turned to face me. I had snatched Dime up and had the knife to his throat. Ashley still rocked back and forth. I sawed until Dime's body dropped to the floor. I still held his head in my arm. Nitti's mouth formed a big O as if he was trying to yell, No! But his tongue was gone. I threw Dime's head in Ashley's lap. She grabbed the head, crawled to Dime's body and tried to put it back on.

"Mama gonna fix it, baby, just be still!" Ashley said.

Every time she tried to put his head on his neck, it rolled off. I walked up behind her with the silenced .45 and blew her brains out.

"You touched the wrong grandmama, nigga," I said to Nitti as I put the gun to the back of his head and pulled the trigger until I could look through his head and see the bloody floor.

I took the cuffs and ties off of them and brought everything to the bathroom, where I cleaned up. I put another dress on, fixed my hair bows, and put everything in the Tape City bag. I went outside, got on my Barbie bike, and rode away. A few blocks over, I pushed the bike into someone's yard, got in my car, changed clothes and drove off.

I know what y'all are thinking … I didn't have to do all that. If niggas violate my family, everybody must go. I'll be waiting, Man!

Chapter 10

Man

"Brown, get ready for court!" the jailer yelled.

I still had on the shitty jumpsuit. I stretched and turned around. The janitor came through and looked at me. He was a guy I went to school with, who became one of my customers. Without saying a word, he dropped his head and set the newspaper on the bars. I picked the paper up, and in bold letters were the words, TRIPLE HOMICIDE. Nitti's face stood out first, then his girl, then … oh shit!

I threw the newspaper down, fell to the floor and balled up in a knot. One side of my brain was telling me to kill everyone, and the other side was saying, *kill yourself.*

The jailers came to get me with their noses turned up. My cell smelled like straight shit. I got up and turned around to be cuffed. The jailers led me to a patrol car and rolled down the windows before they got in. I didn't care. I don't have nobody. I listened as the jailers talked about the murders.

"Whoever it was wasn't playing. They cut the baby's head off!" the jailer said.

I had to pee and didn't feel like holding it, so I just pissed on myself. I've lost everyone, and now I'm about to go to prison. I don't even give a fuck anymore. We pulled up at the courthouse. No one was there taking pictures this time, and I didn't care if they were.

I was led straight to the courtroom. The victim's side was full of white people. The old retired judge sat at the front staring at me. No one was sitting on my side. I was hoping Auntie and Nitti would walk through the door. My lawyer came through the side door and sat beside me. He looked at me and frowned.

"What the fuck did you do, shit on yourself?" he asked.

I heard a lot of talking, but I was in my own world until the judge called my name for the third time.

"Sir," I said loud enough for him to barely hear me.

The smell of shit filled the courtroom. The white people frowned and fanned their noses.

"Do you understand that you're entering an open plea?" the judge asked.

"Yes, sir."

"Alright, for the murder of Sarra Moore, I sentence you to one hundred and twenty months to one hundred and eighty months in the department of public safety."

I looked at my lawyer.

He stared at the judge in shock then hopped up.

"Your Honor, may I approach the bench?" Tommy asked.

"Yes, you may."

I sat there in shock. They had tricked me into pleading guilty and then gave me ten to fifteen years!

Tommy came back to the table shaking his head.

"I'm sorry, Man, they put some shit in the game. I'll file an appeal. You're still two and a half million to the good with me."

I looked back and saw Sarra's uncle smiling at me. I threw my chair back. The jailer was waiting for me to act up. He shot me in the back with the taser. All of those volts shot through my body, making me shit on myself again. The white people left the courtroom holding their noses. The jailers dragged me out to the patrol car. They wouldn't even let me go get my property. The jailers drove me straight to Central Prison in Raleigh, North Carolina.

Soon as I got there, they made me take the shitty clothes off and get in the shower. I know how a baby feels when he wants to be changed. The correctional officer escorted me to the nurse's station, then to talk to the psychologist. I wasn't trying to talk to her. She gonna ask me am I depressed after they done gave me ten years for some shit that I didn't even do. She got mad because I wouldn't talk, and told them to get me out of her office. Little did she know, I have enough money in the bank and in a safe deposit box to have her whole family killed.

The officer took me to a cell and locked me in. A trap door sat in the middle of the metal door. The correctional officer (CO) asked for my clothes, even my socks and boxers. I thought he was gonna give my shit back. He closed the trap door and walked off.

"Yo ... yo!" I yelled.

He came back to the door. "What's up, man?" he asked, looking like Martin Luther King, Jr.

"Why are you taking my clothes?" I asked, standing there naked.

"You can't have them, you're in mental health."

I walked away from the small window on the door. A thick blanket lay on the bed. There were no sheets, just a plastic mattress. I looked up, and a camera was behind a plexiglass window aimed at me. I felt so weak, I didn't know what to do. I knew I had to show these people that nothing was wrong with me so I could get to a phone.

Two months later, a CO escorted me to regular population. I was so happy to get away from all of them crazy people. I walked in the block and ran to the phone. I dialed a number that I would never forget.

"Hello," the man answered in a muffled voice.

"You have a collect call from, Man. Press five to accept, or hang up."

He pressed five.

"You gotta help me!" I said.

"I read about you in the paper. You killed a retired judge's niece. What the fuck were you thinking?" he said.

"She dove out of my car and told them that I pushed her out, all because I told her it was over. Do you think I'm that sloppy? You've seen my work."

"I can't help you on this one, but …"

"Listen, you cracker ass motherfucker!" I said, cutting him off. "Either you get this extra time off of me, or I'll tell everything!" I yelled.

"You were supposed to finish the job. It's not done."

"You said after she goes to college, that's two years from now. I'm a man of my word!"

"Let me make some calls. Give me your lawyer's number. Never mind, I'll just call my brothers," he said and hung up.

I looked around. Everyone was staring at me. I went to my cell and fixed my bunk up.

Chapter 11

Grandma Towns

Man done lost his goddamn mind! He got all that damn money, he looks good and got some good ass dick. Lord, I got to fan my pussy. His stupid ass wants to go kill a white girl. I know he'll call soon. I can't turn my back on him. I know I used to fuck him and Johnny, but somehow I love them like my kids also. Call me nasty or whatever, but this is my goddamn pussy, and if I want to give it away, I can.

All this damn killing going on around here. I wonder who killed my baby? I miss her so much. Sometimes I look at Keba and see Cassandra's face. It's a sad situation to have to bury your child. Thinking of Keba, her mother's death is the only reason I haven't kicked her li' nasty ass. I had not done the laundry, and I was looking through her drawer for some socks and found about twenty-six sex toys and a CD. I pulled the CD out and put it in the DVD player.

Keba and her nasty friend, Tracy, were fucking the hell out of sissy boy next door. I started to beat her ass black. The next thing I know, my hand was in my pussy. I was laying on Keba's bed rubbing my clit. Keba letting that boy cum on her face brought me back to reality. My God, what is getting into these kids? I put the disk back in the same spot. I want her to trust me, so I'll keep this to myself, but her ass is getting on the pill. I held up her eight-inch vibrator, dropped it back in the drawer, and closed it. She is not gonna fuck her life up like her mother. I'll kill her ass first. I gotta go on the porch and get some air.

Look at Jean going in the house. I don't see how the fuck she take that big dick Johnny got every damn night. That man got enough dick for three men. He used to have my pussy crying. Damn, I'm getting wet again. I got to find me another man. This motherfucker I'm with just ain't enough. I wonder if Jason can handle this pussy. No, I can't do my baby like that. Let me go call my man to see what he is doing. He might squeeze me in for a quickie.

Chapter 12

Man

6 months later ...

"Brown, get ready for your visit!" the CO yelled.

I hopped up. Who the fuck was coming to see me? Fuck a shower, brushing teeth, all that. I was happy to see somebody. The only thing I received was a check from the bank each month that my lawyer had set up for me. I rushed out of the block, making the CO walk faster behind me. I went into the booth, and my lawyer sat there smiling. Wasn't shit funny to me. He combed his hair back, then put his comb in his inside jacket pocket.

"What brings you here?" I asked.

"I don't know who you know, but you'll be in court on Monday morning for a resentencing hearing. I'm expecting you'll be getting the three years, as we agreed on at first."

I jumped up screaming. The guard walked to the booth with his stick out and told me to hold it down.

"I'll have you shipped from this place to a medium custody camp after you go to court. That way, you'll be able to get some work release and get a little pussy, maybe."

"Good looking out!"

"Don't thank me, thank whoever you called."

My visit ended and I walked back to the block, happier than I've been in a long time.

Monday ...

I stood in front of the same judge. This time, with a suit on, and smelling like Armani cologne.

"Mr. Brown, do you still enter an open plea?" the judge asked.

"Yes, sir."

"For the death of Sarra Moore, I sentence you to thirty-six to forty-two months in the department of public safety."

My lawyer patted me on the back and smiled like he had done something for me. If he doesn't give me all of my money back on prepaid when I get out, he's a dead man. I shook his hand and walked to the back to be sent back to prison.

Chapter 13

Arkeba

Things have been so crazy around here lately. Grandma is acting real strange, and Jason and Johnny stay gone most of the time. A UPS truck pulled up in front of my house, and since Grandma is gone to her friend's house, I signed for the package. It was addressed to me anyway. No name or letter came with the box. I went to my room and opened the box. There were two envelopes and two VCR tapes inside the box. Soon as I opened the envelopes, my mouth flew open. It was a picture of Grandma with a white man when she was young. He had her in the doggy style position.

I flipped through the pictures. One was of Grandma's pussy. Damn, Grandma got a big, fat meaty pussy! It was scary to me. I continued to flip. The white man fucked her in all different positions, even in the ass. I never even thought about doing that. I opened the other envelope. Damn, Grandma, I didn't know that you get down like that. One was of Grandma standing and talking to Johnny and that guy named Man, who used to come here back in the day. Another was of her coming out the club with Johnny and Man. One showed her going into a hotel with Johnny and Man, and one with her coming out of the hotel with her hair all over the place. The rest were of her going in and out of hotels with different men.

The last five were of my mother letting Johnny and Man in her house, and of them leaving early the next morning. A white girl was in one of the pictures leaving my mom's house as well. It made me wonder if white girls' pussy look and taste like ours. Honestly, it made my cake so wet. I laid their pictures down and put one of the tapes in the VCR.

Grandma, when she was very young, came on the screen. She lay on the bed fucking herself in the ass with an eight and a half inch dildo. She sat all the way down on the dildo, making it disappear in her ass. The white man set the camcorder on the stand, then got on the bed and ate Grandma's pussy while the dildo was up her ass. He pulled her pussy lips open. They looked like the Batman symbol spread open. Her clit was huge. The white man licked and sucked her the way that dyke bitch did me. I couldn't be still. I fast-forwarded the tape, and Grandma had cleaned the dildo off and put it in her pussy. She had her legs pulled back. The man went in her ass, causing her to fuck herself faster with the dildo. I fast-forwarded again, and they were doing all types of nasty shit to each other.

I took that tape out and put the other tape in. My mother appeared. I put my hand over my mouth as tears came to my eyes. She and a kind of tall white guy appeared. His face was blurred. He and my mama did almost the same nasty stuff that Grandma and the other man did. It made me miss my mama! I turned the tape off, balled up, and cried myself to sleep.

I woke up to my grandma calling my name. I got up, took the tape out, and put it in the box with everything else. A picture of a white man in a ... wait, that's the same man that Grandma was with! I tossed everything in the box, ran, and hid it in my closet. Grandma busted into my room, smelling the air. I looked straight at her cake and thought about her huge pussy lips. Not in a freaky way, though.

"What are you doing?" Grandma asked.

"Nothing, about to listen to my radio."

"Drive to the grocery store and get me some flour so I can cook this chicken."

"You just came from past the grocery store, why didn't you stop and get some, and why haven't I met your friend?"

"Don't worry about where I came from, just do what I told you to do. And you'll meet my friend when I get ready for you to meet him!"

"You don't have to be all mean." I got up, put on my Bugs Bunny slippers, and headed out the door.

"Put a damn coat on before you get sick!" she yelled.

I wore a white t-shirt and gray jogging pants. I turned around and grabbed my coat to stop her from running her mouth.

As I drove, I listened to my girl, Lil' Kim, rap about getting fucked. This bitch made my pussy wet just by listening to her. A truck pulled up beside me. I had not paid it any attention. They kept blowing their horn. I looked over there. It was a black Range Rover with 24-inch chrome rims. Three guys were in the truck. One rolled down the window and yelled. I smiled at them as the light turned green, and I took off. Slowing down, I let them get in front of me. Their tags said, New Orleans. I pulled back in front of them and made a right into the grocery store parking lot. They turned in behind me.

I got out of my car and headed toward the store, making my ass jiggle with every step. Me not wearing any panties made it shake even harder. I just wanted to fuck! I turned around and walked back to their truck. The three of them had to be related. They looked almost alike. They were dark skinned, tall and slim, one had dreads, and they all had gold in their mouths.

"I know y'all want some pussy. I got a man, I'm not looking for that, but whoever got the biggest dick can get the pussy."

They pulled their dicks out right there in the grocery store parking lot. When the one in the passenger seat pulled out his dick, I almost lost my breath. I got back in my car and told them to follow me. I drove behind an abandoned house and parked. The one with the big dick got out. By the time he got to my car, I had climbed in the back seat, pulled some condoms out of my purse, and took my sweat pants off. He opened my back door. I lay back and opened my eyes. He was an ugly motherfucker, but his dick was beautiful! He put on a condom and slid into my pussy. I think my mouth got me in trouble. He had twelve inches easy. When he was about nine inches deep, I tried to push him up.

"No … you hurt …no!" I moaned loud.

He didn't hear shit! He slid the other inches in me and fucked me hard. I screamed for dear life. That shit didn't feel good at all. He was fucking me so hard. The other two guys stood looking through my window with their dicks in their hands. The guy fucking me came and pulled out of my pussy. I lay there moaning with my eyes closed.

I heard another condom wrapper being ripped. I opened my eyes and another one had got on top of me. I didn't try to stop him. He pushed my legs back and fucked me hard. This wasn't what I had planned, but I didn't want him to stop. I felt the other guy reach under him and start messing with my asshole. I wanted him to stop, but the other guy felt so good in my cake. I moved and dodged him until he pushed his finger in my ass. I screamed loud, but I don't understand why I didn't ask him to stop. I felt myself cum. Cum ran out of my pussy onto the guy's finger, making it easier for him to penetrate my asshole. The guy in my pussy soon came and pulled out. I was about to turn over, so I could let the other guy fuck me from the back. My asshole felt wet. It kind of felt nasty back there. Both of my holes were throbbing for some more.

My driver's license had fallen on the floor, out of my jogging pants pocket. The big dick one picked it up and read it.

"Yo, this little bitch only sixteen years old!" he said.

The one who had just finished fucking me grabbed my license and looked at it.

"Oh hell naw ... I'm out of here!"

He threw the license on the seat between my legs and ran back to the truck, with Mr. Big Dick behind him. The one with the dreads stood there with his dick in his hand. I looked at him seductively and licked my lips. Them niggas started blowing the horn and backing up slow. He tucked his dick in his pants, ran, and hopped in the truck. I gave them the finger, put my jogging pants back on, got in the front seat, and went to the grocery store. Them niggas were like twenty-five years old and passed up on this wet pussy. They are so fucking wack!

I walked into the house and slammed the flour down on the counter, went to my room and slammed the door. I'm tired of niggas trying to play me like I'm too young. Fuck them. My man doesn't complain. His dick fatter than any of theirs anyway. I picked up the phone to call him.

"Hello," Jason answered.

"Where are you?" I asked.

"I'm at the spot, getting ready to make a drop. What's up?"

"Come over here tonight when you get home."

"All right."

"Listen to this before you hang up." I put the phone on speaker.

My pussy was still wet from earlier. I took two fingers and played with myself until I came. When I picked the phone back up, another guy was talking in the background about how wet my pussy is.

"Who is that?" I asked.

"Oh, that's my man, Lil' T."

"Tell him I said hey, and show him how pretty it is. I'll see you tonight, I love you, baby."

"Love you too."

Chapter 14

Johnny

I'm back, y'all! Richer and wiser than ever. Yeah, my family straight, but we're still stacking paper. I still drive the same Vette, and J-Money still got the Accord. I won't make the same mistakes that I made the last time. Jean opened a Jamaican restaurant in Rocky Mount and a reggae club in Raleigh. Jason and I just bought into a watch company in China that makes watch phones. We're about to open a store in Greensboro that sells all type of watch phones. Yeah, life is good right now. My goal is to be through with this drug shit in two more years. Jason talking about starting a porn company, but I don't know about that. It's his money, he can do what he wants with it. I gotta convince him to wait until he is eighteen years old. Yes, I'm still making his ass go to school.

I pulled my car around the back of the house and started spraying it down with the water hose. I looked at Towns' back porch. She was bent over facing me, letting an old white man fuck her from the back. I know her ass see me looking! Towns backed him in a chair with him still in her pussy. She started riding him at a medium pace. Towns put her hand between them fat pussy lips and jacked on her clit like it was a dick. She leaned back, rode his dick while still moving the meat around her clit in a back and forth motion. She closed her eyes and moaned. Her cum dripped off the white man's balls onto the porch. The old man went limp. He must have cum. Towns lifted up off of him.

Towns crazy as hell! She got some good pussy, though. I finished washing my car and drove around front. I watched the man come out of Towns' house, get in his Cadillac and drive away. Towns watched the car leave, turned toward me, pulled her dress up, and bent all the way over. She rubbed her fingers over her pussy lips and pulled them open. I shook my head and went in the house to take a shower.

While I was in the shower, I received a text from Tiny to come pick up some money from the spot. I'm running out of stash spots again, so it's time to call Mike.

I pulled up to the stoplight around the corner from the spot. A black Crown Vic pulled in front of me, and a gray Lexus L/S 400 pulled up behind me. A man jumped out of each vehicle with masks on and M-16s in their hands. All I could do was ball up. Shells came from everywhere. The last thing I remember is grabbing my chest.

Grandma Towns

I didn't expect that damn Johnny to be home today! He caught me getting some dick from my friend. I had to put on a show like I wasn't surprised to see him. I thought he would come over here and get some after I bent over and played in my pussy for him. That horse dick fucker turned around and went in the damn house. I watched him come out about thirty minutes later, get in his car, and drive away. I will get his ass sooner or later.

As the days go by, I see more and more of Cassandra in Arkeba. The girl is so damn smart though. She makes the A honor roll every time. As long as she does that, I can't complain.

As I sat on the porch, I noticed a guy pull into Johnny's driveway damn near on two wheels. Who the fuck is that pulling into Johnny them driveway like that? I wondered. He got out the car running, and banged on the door.

"They're gone!" I yelled.

"Johnny has been shot. I need to get in touch with them!"

"Where he at?" I asked, running next door to the young guy's car.

"The ambulance just took him to the hospital."

"Wait right here." I ran back to my house and called Jean's cell phone.

"Hello," she answered.

"Meet me at the hospital, Johnny has been shot!" I said and hung up.

I ran back outside and the guy was gone. I got in my car and did everything on the dash to the hospital. By the time I got there, Jason and Arkeba were already there.

"How did y'all beat me here?"

"Someone texted Jason at school and told him," Arkeba said.

I watched Jason pace back and forth like a caged lion. He paced until his mother showed up.

Jean ran in, screaming Johnny's name. Jason grabbed her and held her tight. She cried in his arms. Jean, Jason, Arkeba and I sat quietly, waiting for what seemed like forever before the doctor finally came out of the operating room.

"He made it through surgery. He took seven bullets. His great physical shape stopped the bullets from doing more damage. The most critical wound was to his chest. If he makes it through the next three days, he should be all right."

"Can we see him?"

"I'll give you fifteen minutes."

Jason and Jean went to see Johnny. Three minutes later, Jason walked past Arkeba and I. Arkeba got up to go with him, but I grabbed her arm.

"Jason ... Jason!" Arkeba cried.

"He'll be okay, let him go," I whispered in my grandbaby's ear.

Jason

These bitch niggas done violated! I walked into that hospital room and saw my pops hooked up to all those tubes and it broke me down. I can't see him like that. I guess motherfuckers didn't learn the last time. Tiny had been calling me ever since I left the hospital. I pulled up at the spot in Pinetops. Tiny's car was nowhere in sight. I checked my phone, and the text read, *come to the basement.* I pulled my two nines out and cocked them. As I opened the door slowly, my phone beeped.

"Who the fuck sent y'all?" I heard Tiny yell.

I ran down the steps with my guns pointed. A tall, dark skinned guy lay on the floor hogtied. He was about twenty-four or twenty-five years old, a little over six feet, with dreads and gold in his mouth.

"We saw you pull up!" Tiny said, pointing to the monitors.

"Who is this?" I asked.

"I called Johnny to meet me at the spot in Tarboro to get that money," Tiny began. "He's never late. I heard gunshots and saw Johnny's car down at the intersection. I saw two cars racing away from the scene. I thought that they had kidnapped him, so Lil'T and I followed them. Then, I got a text saying Johnny had been shot, and that the people were taking him to the hospital in an ambulance.

"Lil'T pulled up beside the first car and I shot the driver in the face with my .44. The car went airborne and flipped over. The black Crown Vic got away, but this nigga was in the passenger seat of the other car that flipped."

"So, the nigga won't talk?" I asked.

"We been beating the shit out of him. He won't say a word," Lil'T said.

"Tiny, you got a pocket knife on you?" I asked.

Tiny went into his pocket, pulled out a hawk bill knife, and handed it to me.

"Lil'T, go get a pen and some paper," I said.

Lil'T left and came back with an ink pen and a torn paper bag.

"First, who lives with you, and where do they live?" I asked.

The guy lay on the floor looking up at me. Both of his eyes were almost shut. I opened one of his eyes and pushed the knife's tip into the core. He screamed like a bitch. I pulled the knife out of his eye socket slowly, bringing his eyeball out on the tip of the knife. Blood ran out like a faucet.

"Now, I'll ask you again, who?"

"Mane, I'm not even from down here. I'm from New Orleans. My cousin told me that we had to put in some work so we could get a connect!"

"Where do your cousin live?" I asked.

"One is my cousin. My brother was killed, and my other brother is at my cousin's house."

"Where do y'all stay?"

"1312 Hunter Street, in Rocky Mount."

"What's their names?"

"My brother name is John-John, and my cousin name is Color."

"I know the nigga, Color. He the one who snitched on my man, Power, from Rocky Mount," Lil'T said.

"Mane, I know y'all gonna let me go!"

"Who was gonna be your connect?"

"Some nigga named Man, that's locked up."

"You're a rat ass nigga. I guess your family is just alike. I don't like rats."

I stuck the knife in his other eye and popped his eyeball out. Blood ran from both eye sockets. He lay on the floor screaming that he couldn't see.

"Bring me some pliers!"

Tiny went into his toolbox and handed me some pliers. I stuck them in the nigga's mouth and clamped his tongue. I pulled it until it wouldn't come out any further, then I stuck the knife deep into his mouth and cut his tongue out. Blood spilled out of his mouth as he tried to talk, but a man with no tongue can't say shit. I took the end of the knife, shoved it in his ear, turned the knife, and snatched meat out of his ear, along with his eardrum. I went to the other ear and did the same thing. He passed out on the floor as Tiny and Lil' T looked at me like I was crazy.

"Y'all chop this motherfucker's hands off."

I drove to the stash spot and came back with an AK-47. Lil' T and I loaded the nigga in the car. The ride to Rocky Mount was quiet. We finally got to Hunter Street, where a black Range Rover and black Crown Vic sat in the yard in front of the address. Tiny dropped me and the guy off down the street from the house. He staggered weakly from losing so much blood. I grabbed him and pushed him to the door, then ran behind their Range Rover with the AK strapped around my shoulder.

The door opened, and two guys ran outside to the guy who was laid out. I came up behind them and shot their asses down. Standing over them, I gave them head shots. A girl ran to the door screaming. I shot her ass down too. I left the blind nigga alive so niggas will know what will happen if they cross us again. I ran down the street, hopped in the car with Lil' T and Tiny.

Tiny fired up a cigar and pulled off laughing.

"What's so funny?" I asked.

"Can't nobody tell me that Johnny ain't your daddy."

"I'm a gangster by birth, not by choice."

"I hear you, young blood!"

Chapter 15

Man

I had been moved to a camp called Eastern Correctional. I like this shit! My own room, laid back on the cell phone, with a bitch on both shifts. Pussy, money, food, drugs, all that! I took my phone off the charger and powered it on. Two texts came through. Oh, shit! Oh, shit! They got that nigga.

I had met Color in here. He was about to go home. All he wanted to do was make some money. I told him that I would put him on if he killed Johnny. Johnny is gone now! I lay back on my bed and smiled as I dialed my out of state connect. I gotta turn this nigga on, I owe him big time. When my connect didn't answer, I checked the other text.

My cousin is missing, the text said.

I hate to tell him, but that nigga is probably dead. The money he will be making soon will help him forget about that nigga.

"Brown, you have a case manager visit," CO Arnold said.

She is brown skinned, twenty-seven years old, on the tall side, with a fat ass. I followed Arnold out of the block and down the hallway. She looked back to see if anyone was around, then turned into the bathroom. I went in behind her. The door automatically locked. I pushed her to the wall and tongue kissed her. She unbuckled her belt and pulled two vacuum sealed packages out, which contained a half pound of exotic weed. I turned her around, pulled her pants and panties down, then pulled my pants down. I could smell her musk from walking all day. It turned me on. Ain't nothing like a sweaty pussy.

I went in Arnold's pussy from the back. Her shit stayed so tight. I pounded away in her pussy until it started drying up. I soon came, looking at her pretty shaped ass. She reached around, grabbed the tissue, and wiped her pussy. Then she turned around, squatted and licked the cum off my dick. Arnold fingered herself while she sucked and moaned.

"It's ready now, bae," Arnold said, looking up at me.

I sat on the toilet and she turned her back to me, reached under, grabbed my dick, and guided it into her pussy. It was soaking wet. She bounced up and down on my dick, trying hard to hold in her moans. I felt her cumming on my dick. She turned around, licked it off, then stood up. Arnold reached for the tissue, but I stopped her.

"I want you to feel my nut running in your panties until you get home."

"Boy, you crazy." She smiled and pulled her panties up. "I'll bring the other half for you when I come back to work."

I went in my pants and gave her a thousand dollars. Arnold folded the money and put it in her pocket. She opened the door and walked out. Arnold went in one direction and I went in the other, with the weed tucked in my pants. I bagged up all ounces for five hundred dollars an ounce. I already had half of it sold. I'm starting to like this prison shit. I went to the shower then to the card table. During count time, I tried to call my nigga, Color, but his shit kept going to voicemail. I went on Facebook for a while, then laid it down.

My other chick, Stanley, woke me up early the next morning. I was mad as fuck! She is a red-bone and put you in the mind of a light-skinned Jennifer Hudson before she lost weight, with blond hair.

"What's up?" I asked, standing at the door in my boxers.

"You heard about your boy?" she asked.

"Which one?"

"Color!" Officer Stanley said and handed me the Rocky Mount Telegram.

On the front page in bold letters was the headline, "FOUR GUNNED DOWN AND ONE TORTURED."

I dropped my head. I know them bitch niggas gave me up. I closed the door in her face and lay down. She stared at me for a minute through the window then walked off.

If Johnny is gone, who the fuck is putting in work like that? I grabbed the newspaper and looked for Johnny's shooting. It had a small clipping at the bottom of the paper. *Tarboro man, Johnny Bullock, was gunned down yesterday. He is in critical condition at Heritage Hospital.* This motherfucker won't die!

"Yard call!" Officer Stanley yelled.

I eased into my clothes, brushed my teeth, and went outside. I pulled my shirt jacket over my ears, made two rounds around the yard, and went back in the block. Officer Stanley blew a kiss at me as I walked past. I walked back to my room, looked in the corner, and smiled. A brown paper bag sat in the corner. I went straight to the bag. Ten cell phones were in there. I had seven of the fifteen-dollar phones sold for five hundred dollars apiece. I walked past the old Indian guy's room, dropped the phone, and kept walking back out of the block.

The bathroom door was cracked. Stanley stood peeping out, waiting for me. I looked around and slipped into the bathroom. I handed her one thousand dollars, and she went straight to her knees, unbuttoned my pants, and put my dick in her mouth. Her wet mouth warmed my dick instantly. Stanley shined my dick like new marble. She sucked and jacked at the same time. I stood on my tiptoes. This bitch is a porn star, I swear. Stanley slowed up, wrapped her lips around my dick, grabbed my cheeks, and pulled me deep down her throat. I moved in and out of her mouth. She cupped my balls and massaged them. I began to cum. Tears came to the corner of my eyes as I exploded in her mouth.

Stanley eased up off of my dick and sucked it real slow, bringing it back to life. She stood up, unbuckled her belt, turned around, and slid her bloomers and pants down. Her big fat juicy ass stood out. I went up in her pussy from the back. She threw it back to me hard. Her ass was so fat, it was knocking me all over the bathroom. I pushed her all the way over and fucked her hard and deep. My thighs clapped against her ass. I grabbed her long blond hair and came in her pussy. She looked at me in the mirror over the sink, reached back, pulled my dick out of her pussy, and rubbed it against her asshole.

"Do she let you put it in there?"

I couldn't talk, all I could do was shake my head no. She pushed the head in her ass, moaned, and pulled it back out. My dick was back hard instantly. She moved her hand up and down my dick.

"You be a good boy, and you might get it next time."

Stanley let my dick go, grabbed the tissue, and wiped her pussy. I stood there with my pants down, staring at her fat juicy ass.

"So you gonna leave me like this?" I asked.

"We gotta save some for her, don't we?"

She slicked down her hair and walked out of the bathroom. I pulled my pants up, grabbed the cleaning supplies, and walked. Damn, I got it good. Money will make a bitch do anything ... HA! HA! HA!

Chapter 16

Jason

After school, Keba and I drove straight to the hospital. I didn't go into the room where Johnny was. I can't look at him like that. Keba and my mama sat in the room with him. After a while, they came and gave me an update on Johnny.

"He's breathing on his own now. The doctor said he may have to go through a little physical therapy, but he'll be all right," Ma said.

A tear came to the corner of my eye. I tried to hold it in, but it won the battle and rolled down my cheek. Johnny had just come into my life; I wasn't ready to lose him that fast.

"It's okay, baby. He's strong," Mama said.

"Tell him I handled that, and I just can't see him like he is. Tell him things will be ready when he get out."

Keba came around the corner with food for everyone. We sat and ate, then I kissed my mama and left.

Keba is my baby, but Pops always told me not to take anyone to our stash spots. I dropped her off at home, made drop offs, and pickups, like Pops had taught me. Shit ain't adding up about these dudes that got at Pops. I dropped the last money off at the stash house. I wondered how the fuck did them niggas know what type of car Johnny was driving, and how they know that he was going to make a pickup. Somebody is sour!

I drove to the spot that Tiny ran, went into the house, and flopped down on the couch.

"Is there anything that you missed or forgot to tell me?" I asked Tiny.

"It was a guy at the spot when we got there."

"How did he look?"

"Kind of brown-skinned, and 'bout five-nine, one eighty, close haircut. He usually is there when I meet Johnny.

"You're talking about Lil' Tony?"

"I think that's him."

I walked out the door immediately, got in my car, and drove to the other spot. I can't believe this nigga would betray us. We took good care of our workers. I pulled up and hopped out of my car. The guys we had guarding the spot followed me into the house.

"Yo, Tony, tell me how did niggas know what my pops was driving and that he was coming to pick up!" I yelled, pulling out my Beretta Nine.

"I didn't want to tell you this, but when I saw the newspaper and saw that black Range Rover with the New Orleans plates, it came to me that your girl was standing in the grocery store parking lot talking to them niggas. She didn't go in. She got back in her car, and they followed her," Lil' Tony said.

"My girl, who?"

"The mixed chick with the 740."

"Why the fuck you didn't tell me that shit?"

"You said that's your girl, but you have an open relationship, so I didn't think anything of it."

I wanted to kill that nigga bad, but them niggas in the spot were closer to him than me. I couldn't trust that. Without saying anything else, I jumped in my car and sped home. Ms. Towns' car wasn't there. I walked in without knocking. Keba had just got out of the shower.

"Boy, you scared me. Don't be doing that shit!" she said, putting her hand to her chest.

I slapped her ass to the floor. She grabbed the side of her face, jumped up and started swinging. I pulled out my gun and put it between her eyes.

"Bitch, you better give me some answers and some good ones."

"What are you talking about?" Keba cried.

"Who the fuck were the guys in the black Range Rover that you met at the grocery store?"

"They pulled up, trying to holla at me. I don't know who the fuck they were," she screamed.

"And then what?"

"I decided to give them some pussy, and that's it!"

I slapped her stupid ass to the floor again. "Because of your hoe ass, my pops is in the hospital fucked up. Did you know that those are the niggas that shot him?"

"No, I didn't know!" she said, getting up off the floor.

"Tell me what went down, and if you leave out anything, I'll blow your fucking face off!"

"They followed me to the grocery store. I went to their truck and told them that I have a man, but one of them could get the pussy with the biggest ... anyway, I let them follow me to an abandoned house. I fucked two of them. It was three altogether. One of them got my driver's license off the floor and saw my age. They stopped fucking me and left. I swear on my life! How could you think I would betray you?"

"Bitch, you did, by fucking my enemies. Your hoe ass got to get fucked by every dick you see!"

"Jason, you're hurting right now. Get that gun out of my face!"

"Fuck that, somebody going to give me some answers!"

"Well, I don't have any for you!"

"Don't even worry about it, hoe ass bitch!"

I stormed out the door.

"Jason ... Jason," she screamed over and over.

I got in my car and went looking for somebody to fuck up for my pops getting shot. I passed Grandma Towns going home. She waved. I kept going.

Grandma Towns

I walked into my house and saw that all of my shit was turned over. I tip-toed into my room, got my damn double barreled shotgun, then tip-toed to Arkeba's room. She lay on her bed crying.

"What happened, baby?" She looked up at me. "Who the fuck hit you in your face?"

I was so mad! She had a handprint on her jaw and eye.

"Jason and I got into a fight! He accused me of setting his daddy up. I would never do him like that!" Keba cried.

"Why would he do that?"

"I met the guys that did it, and he said Man had something to do with the shi … stuff. So he thinks I was in on it."

"Man, who?"

"The one who came here that time. The one that you slapped."

My fucking mind went blank. That sorry bastard set my grandbaby and me up. I knew he wasn't just calling out of the blue. He kept asking me questions about Johnny. I didn't know they had beef like that, so I told him that Johnny lived beside me, and still drove the same Corvette from back in the day. I even sent that sorry motherfucker some pictures of my pussy to his phone. They must have been following Johnny. What got me pissed off is that motherfucker included my grandbaby in this shit. I remember telling him what kind of car she drives. That motherfucker!

I went into the kitchen and got my baby some ice to put on her jaw.

"It's gonna be all right, baby," I said.

"No, it's not. Jason hates me!" Keba cried.

"He doesn't hate you. Give him a chance to calm down."

I couldn't tell her that this shit is all my fault. Some shit you gotta take to the grave with you. I went to my room, closed the door, and dialed Man's number.

"What's up, fat pussy?" he answered laughing.

"Why you do that shit to Johnny?" I asked with an attitude.

"He killed all the people that I love, so I tried to have him killed!"

"Why did you include me and my grandbaby in this shit?"

"Your grandbaby included herself. She just like you and Cassandra, can't turn no dick down. They told me that they had just fucked a young girl, driving the car you described to me. I told them to follow her and see if a black Corvette sat in the yard next door. They started watching Johnny's house and car. They even watched you bend over and play with your pussy on the front porch." He laughed.

"Fuck you, motherfucker! I hope you die in there, bitch!" I hung up.

I can't believe this nigga! I gotta talk to Jason, I owe him that much. I dialed the number over and over, but he would not pick up. He probably thought I was Keba calling because I know she was blowing his phone up. Damn, I let that punk ass nigga play me!

Jason

I drove back to the hospital with the weight of the world on my shoulders. I had to be around somebody that I could trust. That shit hurt me that Keba would do some shit like that to me. Y'all don't know how bad I wanted to kill her ass. I made a U-turn to go back to my spot. That's me and my pop's shit. If the nigga Lil' Tony had told me what was good, Pops probably wouldn't be in the hospital. I pulled up in front of the spot and got out. All the gunmen followed me inside again. Lil' Tony sat at the table counting money.

"What's good, J-Money?" he asked, coming into the front room where I was.

"Because you didn't tell me or my Pops what you saw, he's lying in a hospital bed. I can't tolerate shit like that. So, you're no longer on this team. Pack your shit and get the fuck out!"

"Jay … I …"

"You got five minutes, and a half minute just passed, "I said, cutting him off.

I sat and waited for this nigga to pack his shit. It had been seven minutes now. He thinks I'm playing with him. Five minutes later, he walked in the front room.

"I told you that you had five minutes," I said.

He looked at me with a frown, then grilled me.

I looked at my three shooters. I had to test them to see who they were with. Pulling three quarters out of my pocket, I told them to flip the coin. Two landed on head and one on tails. I looked at Mouse and smiled. He is nineteen years old, brown skinned, 5'9" and on the slim side, with ears and face like a mouse.

"You just got a higher position, but first, kill this nigga!" I said.

Mouse pointed his gun with no hesitation and shot Lil' Tony in the face. Lil' Tony fell to the floor kicking, as blood leaked out of his forehead.

"You know your job description. Make Johnny proud."

"I won't let y'all down," he said, as he bent down and took Lil' Tony's jewelry and money.

I walked out of the spot, got in my car, and went to the hospital. I still couldn't get what Keba had done out of my head. I knew she was fucking. It's just them niggas used her to get to my pops, and she wasn't smart enough to see through that. Who is gonna be next, me? I gotta cut her loose.

I went straight to the waiting room. I knew my mama would come out sooner or later. I didn't want to see my pops until he could roll his ass out of that place. About forty minutes later, my mama walked by, drinking coffee.

"Ma!" I yelled.

I ran and hugged her tight.

"What's wrong, baby?" she asked.

"It's nothing. I'll talk to you about it later," I said, letting her go. "How's Pops?"

"He's talking now. I gave him your message. He just said, 'go to school.' "

"Tell him I'm going. I'll be sitting out here for a while."

"Okay, baby, let me go check on your father."

She kissed my jaw and walked to the room.

Arkeba

I should've known that it was more to this story! Grandma didn't even really blank, and she always told me when I get older, never let a man put his hands on me. I heard her on the phone talking and calling Man's name. When I put my ear to the door, I heard everything she said. I tiptoed away from her door, back to my room. I didn't know what to say or do, so I put on one of Jason's t-shirts, a pajama bottom, and my Bugs Bunny slippers. I left the tapes under my pillow, took the two envelopes of pictures, and walked softly out of the house to my car. I drove to both spots that Jason be at and didn't see his car. I dialed Jason's number the whole time.

I decided to go to the hospital. If he wasn't there, I knew that he would show up there sooner or later. I took the elevator up to the seventh floor and walked to the waiting room. Jason sat on the couch with his head back, asleep. I sat across from him, watching his face. I love this boy so much. If he leaves me, I don't know what I will do.

Jason turned his face toward me and opened his eyes as I wiped my tears away. He jumped up. "What the fuck are you doing here?" he almost yelled.

"I have to talk to you. Something ain't right."

"Yeah, you ain't right."

"Just give me ten minutes, and if you don't see what I see, then I'll leave you alone forever!"

"Ten minutes, come on!" He grabbed my arm roughly and pulled me all the way to the stairway.

Jason looked at his watch. "Start talking!"

"Before I say this, promise me that you won't harm my grandmother."

"Nine minutes."

"Do you remember the man that came to Grandma's house?" Jason was silent, but his stare said it all. "His name is Man. That's who is responsible for your pops getting shot."

"And how do you know this?"

"After he came to our house, I had asked Grandma about him, but she played it like he was just an old friend."

"Pops said the same thing."

"The other day, I got these and two VCR tapes in the mail, with no return address." I handed him one envelope.

Jason flipped through the pictures, stopping at the picture of Grandma's pussy.

"What your grandma and this cracker got to do with my pops?" he asked.

"Keep flipping," I said.

He flipped through the pictures until he came to my grandmother in that catsuit. He stopped and looked at her pussy print again, then flipped real fast. He came to the picture of my grandma, Man, and Johnny coming out the club together. The next picture was of them going into a hotel, and the next one was of them coming out. The last picture was the white man in a casket.

"What the fuck!" Jason said.

"I don't know. I'm trying to figure this shit out myself. Now this is what I had to tell you about my grandma. Jason, I love you and you know that's all the family I have. Promise me that you won't hurt her after I tell you this."

"I promise," Jason said.

"After our fight, she came home and found me crying. I told her what had happened, and she didn't even get mad. Grandma left the room and came back with some ice. After she had calmed me down, she went to her room and shut the door. I was going to show her the pictures and tapes, but I heard her say Man and Johnny's name. I put my ear to the door and heard her say, 'why you do that to Johnny?' Then I heard, 'why did you include me and my grandbaby in your shit?' He must have said something crazy, 'cause then she said, 'I hope you die in there.' Oh, check these out."

I handed Jason the envelope. He flipped through the pictures of my mama with the white man with his face blurred out.

"All this shit is crazy," Jason said. "So the guys that met you at the grocery store was a setup?"

"I guess so, I don't know." I began to cry. "I have always told you the truth. I can't control how I am when it comes to that, but I will never betray you over no dick or anyone."

"Come here," Jason said, pulling me into his arms.

"Do you forgive me?"

"Yeah, but from now on, if a nigga or bitch want the pussy, they gotta get recorded. If they're not trying to do that, they can't get none of this."

He grabbed my cake and tongue kissed me. Damn, he can make me so wet.

"We gotta go see your grandmama. She gotta tell us something. We won't show her the pictures. These are our safety net until we find out what's going on."

He grabbed my hand and we walked down the stairs. I think I learned my lesson. I'm not fucking up again. Y'all don't know how I felt … well, some of y'all do.

Grandma Towns

Lord, this damn girl done snuck out of this house! She could've at least told me she was leaving. Hold on, let me catch my breath. I'm feeling nice right now. I went to the liquor store and got me something to sip on, and stopped down the street and bought a bag of weed. This weed these young folks smoke is some serious shit. Damn if I ain't paranoid. I usually just drink and smoke on special occasions, but that damn Man done worked my nerves bad. I got to put this shit out. It's fucking with the nerves in my clit.

Who the fuck is out there? I looked out my window and saw Jason and Keba getting out of their cars and walking to the house. Us Towns girls' pussy is crack and heroin mixed, do y'all hear me? Keba done put it on that boy. I guess the apple don't fall far from the tree.

"Grandma, you've been smoking weed, and you're drinking," Keba said, fanning her nose.

"Can I enjoy myself some damn time? Don't come in here blowing my high!"

"We need to speak with you," Jason said.

"I already know what y'all want. Y'all kids these days stay in grown people business too damn much. I'll tell y'all what you need to know, and not what you want to know." Jason frowned. "Don't frown at me, I'll still tear your little black sissy ass up!"

"Grandma, what's going on around here?" Keba asked.

"Listen, 'cause I was supposed to take this to my grave, and so was Johnny and Man. I met Man and Johnny in the club. I broke their virginity. Them two boys had some dicks on them, wow!" I fanned my pussy.

"Grandma!" Keba yelled, bringing me back to the present.

"We got close, but I was closer to Johnny until he got locked up. Word on the street was that Man and that white girl he killed set Johnny up. After Johnny got locked up, Man started stopping by all the time. He had been around them freaks so long that he started wanting my ass more than this good pussy!"

"Oh my God, I can't believe she is talking like this!" Keba said, embarrassed.

"Anyway, don't interrupt me no God damn more! Through the years, Man slowed up coming around. He popped up after the funeral. The next day, I read in the paper that he had killed the white girl. So, he finally called me. Yeah, I sent him some pictures of my pussy and we had phone sex. He started asking me how everybody was doing, so I told him. I didn't think that motherfucker would hurt Johnny! Then he got me and my baby involved. He had them niggas follow her back here so they could watch Johnny. On my life, I wouldn't hurt Johnny!" I began to cry.

I couldn't hold it in. That damn weed got me emotional.

Jason walked out of the house and slammed the door. I should've told him how his mama ate my pussy! He can be mad at me all he wants, as long as he forgives my grandbaby. I've never seen her hurt like that. She loves that boy, with his damn ugly self.

Jason

Damn, that's where Case and Keba get that freaky shit from. I should go back and make her tell me everything. She didn't even mention that damn white man. She's not telling me something. I wonder why somebody would send Keba those pictures, and I can only imagine what's on those tapes. My phone ringing brought me out of my thoughts.

"Hello," I answered.

"Yo, bruh, my man, Corey, called me and told me that nigga Man called him, trying to cop a pound of loud. Corey asked me could he trust Man because the nigga said the CO bitch was coming to get it," Lil' T said.

"Follow her after she comes to cop. Text me her address and name."

"I got you. How's bruh doing?"

"He's doing better."

"Tell him I send my love. Hit me later."

I walked in the house. Not seeing my mama and Johnny there doing something together made me drop down on the couch, depressed. How the fuck can I get to that nigga Man? He's in prison, still doing bullshit! My phone rang. I looked at it and saw Lil' T's number.

"What's going on?" I answered.

"She's coming tomorrow. Where the hoes at, nigga?" Lil' T asked.

Something came to me and I burst out laughing.

"Come to the house beside my house right now. Pop a Viagra, because she's freaked out!"

"Say no more, I'm on my way."

I hung up and burst out laughing. His ass is in for a treat when he get here. I called Keba and asked her to ride with me to the hospital. She was more than happy to get out of the house.

I heard Grandma Towns say, "Keba, I remember you shitted on yourself when you were five. I burned your ass up!" Grandma Towns burst out laughing.

Keba hung up.

I watched her walk from her house over to my house. She walked in mad.

"Hold up, shitty, let me get my hat." I laughed.

"That shit ain't funny! She over there walking around in some bloomers, no shirt or bra on, barefoot, with an unlit joint in her hand! Why are you smiling?"

"No reason, let's go pick Tracy up," I said on the way to my car.

"I don't care, I'll call her."

Keba and I pulled up in front of Tracy's house. She came out in a pink Polo jacket with the Polo sign in purple, blue tight jeans, and pink and purple Jordans. I stared at her until she got into the car.

"Damn, you're looking good! You got our man waiting to hit that." Keba laughed.

"He know he can get it when he want it," Tracy said, rubbing my braids and looking at the side of Keba's face.

Keba, Tracy, and I went to Rocky Mount and ate at my mama's restaurant, then went to the hospital. We stayed there, talking to my mama for a while. Ma watched Tracy and Keba kiss me before she went to check on Johnny.

Ma came back an hour later. Both of the girls were laid on my shoulder asleep. Ma called my name as I was dozing off. I opened my eyes and she gave me the come here gesture. I moved the girls to the side and went to talk to her. Ma stopped me around the corner.

"What's with you and them two girls?" she asked.

"Keba is my girl, and Tracy is our girl."

"What? Never mind, just be safe alright?"

"Alright, Ma, I gotta go."

Chapter 17

Johnny

I can't believe that I slipped like that! I let this motherfucker catch me slipping! Got me laid up in here all shot up and shit. This nigga gonna pay for this! Let me tell y'all what happened yesterday. This white nurse, she's about twenty-four years old, medium height and slender, with brown hair and brown eyes. I don't know what's in this medicine they got me taking, but it be having my dick hard. Yesterday, the nurse came in. Jean was sitting beside me talking, and my dick was sticking straight up in the air.

"Mr. Bullock, you have to keep your arm elevated over your head or by your chest," the nurse said.

She grabbed my dick! Once she realized that she was trying to pull my dick to my chest, her whole face turned red. She apologized and walked out of my room. Jean could not stop laughing. I laughed for a while until my chest started hurting. That made me think about how this nigga tried to kill me after I let him live. I go home tomorrow, even though I can't do nothing but lay up in the house. Jean has been holding a nigga down for real. When I get out of here, I'm gonna ask her to marry me. I gotta heal first.

J-Money is every spit of me, even though he look like my

mama. I don't want my little man to be out there in them streets, but he didn't choose the streets, the streets chose him. I still gotta stay on him about school. I don't know what him and Arkeba got going on, but I'm staying out of that. I know he'll be happy to see me tomorrow.

The medicine is kicking in. I gotta go.

Jason

I had something to do before the jewelry store closed. I dropped Tracy off, then dropped Keba off. Grandma Towns came to the door smiling and waving at me. I can swear I saw her lips say, thank you. Keba popped her mouth and went into the house.

I drove off and turned my system up. "Many Men," by 50 Cent bumped through my woofers. The song had me in a trance. Next thing I know, I was parking on Main St. in front of the jewelry store. I got out and went in the store. A tall white man stared at me like I was trying to steal something. I walked to the glass case and spotted a ring with ice all around it.

"I'm Chuck, can I help you with something?"

"Can I see that ring right there?" I said, pointing to the ring I wanted.

Chuck stared at my pinky ring. "Nice ring, where did you get that?" he asked as he took the ring out of the case.

"My girl gave it to me for my birthday. Now I gotta get her something nice."

"She'll love this one," he said, handing me the ring.

The price said $7,550. "I bet she will!" I said, staring at the price. "I'll take it."

"You want to put an inscription on it?"

"Yes, put Jay and Keba."

He walked away and came back a few minutes later, still staring at my ring.

"She bought that ring you got on from here. Just give me $5,000.00. Be sure to tell her I gave you a deal."

Damn, Keba done gave him some pussy too! "Yeah, thanks for the deal," I said and paid for the ring.

I snatched the bag and walked out the door. I got in my car and drove back home. After I took a shower, I called Keba over. She arrived ten minutes later. I sat in the front room in some basketball shorts and no shirt.

"Wait!" She stopped at the door. "Close the door and take off all of your clothes right there."

Keba didn't say a word. She took her clothes off as she stared into my eyes. I don't know why I did it, but I stepped out of my shorts so I would be naked too. I grabbed the box off the table, got down on one knee in front of her, and looked up into her eyes.

"I know that we are young and have a lot of growing to do, but I give you this ring as a token of my love for you that will never die."

Keba stood there with tears rolling down her face. I placed her hand in mine and put the ring on her finger. She pushed me back on the floor and dove on top of me. She kissed me from my lips down to the tip of each toe. Keba came back up, reached back, and guided my dick into her pussy. She slid up and down as she moaned and sucked my bottom lip. We ended up sexing on the couch, the hall, then my bed until we passed out.

When we woke up, it was 9:32 at night. Keba kissed me, put her clothes on, and went home. After she left, I wondered what happened with Lil' T. I dialed his number.

"What's good, J-Money?" Lil' T asked.

"Did you see the chicks?"

"No, but I met this old head. I think I love that old bitch!"

I almost choked on my spit. "Word up!"

"Yeah, that's the best and prettiest pussy I ever had in my life! Is her car out there now? I'm on my way back to get me some more."

"Keba is her granddaughter. You better not let her find out."

"I got you, but I gotta send you a picture of that pussy."

"Nigga, I don't want to see that shit!"
"Alright, I'll talk to you later."
The house phone rang as soon as I got off with Lil'T.
"Hello," I answered.
"What's his number?" Grandma Towns whispered.

I gave her Lil'T's number and hung up. I heard my phone beep. When I looked at it, it was a picture text from Lil'T of Grandma Towns' pussy. Them pussy lips look fake. I erased that shit out of my phone.

The next morning, I pulled in front of Keba's house and blew the horn. She stuck her head out the door. I yelled for her to drive her car today. She likes to ride with me so she can turn my radio up. Keba got a brand new 740 BMW, and I got an old ass Honda Accord. She's so damn backward. That's my baby, though.

Just as school was about to let out, I got a text with an address that read 1509 Lane St, Kinston, North Carolina. I put the phone up before my teacher caught me. It was time to bring the little girl out.

Chapter 18

Man

I don't know if I want to be happy or mad! This CO bitch, Arnold, is saying that she is two and a half months pregnant. I'm getting old; it's about time I had me a child. I wonder how many other niggas done hit that. Shit, I met her in prison. She claims I'm the first one in prison to hit that, but I don't believe it. The bitch loves money too damn much. She be coming through for a nigga. When she come to work tomorrow, I should be straight. I love the way she treats me though.

Officer Stanley is another story. I love that bitch, 'cause she makes me beg for the pussy, and she so damn freaky. The other day, she told me to sit on the toilet so she could ride me. She bent all the way over, spread her ass cheeks, and finally put my dick in her ass. That bitch squeezed her ass muscles on my dick like she do her pussy. Her shit was already tight. She lifted up off my dick and got down on all fours. Stanley had kicked her shoes off and stepped out of her pants and bloomers. She spread her ass and asked me if I wanted some more.

I got down on the floor to get it, but she wouldn't let me put it in unless I begged. She had me like a bitch, on my knees behind her, begging, with my dick in my hand. She played with her clit while I begged. I watched cum drip out of her pussy and onto her uniform. I couldn't take it anymore. I went up in that ass and didn't come out until I came. She got me gone for real.

My man goes home next month. I'm gonna finish what I started with this nigga, Johnny. I heard he had a son. He gonna get it too! I gotta go, there go officer Stanley. I wonder what she got for me today. She stay cooking me some good shit. Niggas done started hating, but I got a big ass knife. Let them act stupid. I'm gonna show their ass how this country boy blank. North Carolina niggas rather see niggas without shit than with it.

I hope this loud is official. I gotta make some money; that's the only way that I can stay sane.

"Brown, go to the sergeant's office!" Officer Stanley said, looking at my dick print.

Y'all know what time it is, hating ass motherfuckers!

Chapter 19

Jason

It had just got dark when I walked around the corner in a skirt, halter top with little tissue balls stuffed inside, dirty Air Ones, and white hair bows on the end of my braids. I twirled the hula-hoop around my arm in Officer Arnold's driveway. I had already driven by and threw my bag of goodies in her grass. About thirty minutes later, she turned into her driveway. I slipped to the side with the hula-hoop around my waist.

Arnold looked at me and smiled as she got out of her car and went to the door. I picked up the paper bag, pulled the .380 handgun out, and crept up behind her. Arnold opened the door, and I pushed the gun to the back of her neck.

"Bitch, if you scream, I'll blow your whole neck off!" I said through clenched teeth. "Walk. Is anyone else in here?"

"No, please don't kill me!" she said, walking into the house.

I pushed her inside and shut the door. She fell to the floor in tears.

"I got money, and it's a pound of weed in my closet!"

"Do you know Man?"

"Who?"

"Man."

She thought for a minute. "You're talking about Brown. Yes, I know him."

Arnold's phone started ringing and Man's face popped up on the screen. I snatched her phone off the floor and hit ignore, then went through her saved pictures. She had pictures of Man, butt naked, with his dick in his hand. Pictures of herself naked, doing all types of freaky shit, and a picture of her stomach poking out a little. An idea popped in my head.

"What did I do?" she asked.

"You fucked the wrong nigga. Turn around and back up toward me."

She turned around and backed up. I placed the cuffs on her arms, then put the ties on her legs.

"I promise I will leave him alone!"

"He sent me to kill you!"

"Why would he do this to me?" she cried.

"He said that you was having his baby, and he don't want a baby by a whore. How do you think I know that you're pregnant? He told me to cut your baby out."

I went into my bag and pulled out my big Rambo knife.

"Please, no, please!" Arnold cried.

She was so stupid. Once I saw the picture of her stomach, I put two and two together. I lifted her shirt and rubbed the knife against her stomach. She couldn't have had on any panties because piss shot from between her legs onto the floor. She screamed as I put a scratch on her stomach.

"I can't do this to you! You're too pretty to be hurt because you want to be loved," I said, sounding sad that I had come to her.

I put the knife against her ties and cut them off.

"Thank you … thank you … thank you!"

I took the cuffs off her.

She turned around and hugged my neck.

I pushed her away.

"You need to stop fucking with that bitch ass nigga. He doesn't care about you!"

Arnold began to cry louder and flopped on the couch. "I'm having an abortion!"

"Do what you gotta do."

As I turned to walk out of the house, her phone rang. It was Man again. Arnold picked her phone up off the table and put it on speaker.

"Hello!" she answered.

"Why didn't you answer the phone?" Man asked.

"Fuck you, I'm having an abortion!" She hung up and threw her phone against the wall, shattering it.

I went in my bag and gave her five thousand dollars.

"That is what he gave me to kill you."

Arnold took the money and hugged me again. I pulled away from her, picked up my bag and walked out of her house. She started crying again, came to the door, and watched me leave. I took off running soon as I was out of her sight. I ducked through two houses and got in my car. Before I drove off, I changed back into my clothes, took the bows out, and drove off. I had to pick money up and drop off work at the spots.

Chapter 20

Man

Two Weeks Later

"Prepare for breakfast," someone said over the intercom.
    I got up, still mad because this bitch, Arnold, has been missing in action. She has not been to work in two weeks. After handling my hygiene, I went to eat. Oh shit, there that bitch go! She stood in the dining hall, monitoring the inmates. She better have something for me! The search team ran in our block last week, and I had to flush my damn phone. This bitch, Stanley got fired, trying to bring another nigga some phones. Hell yeah, I put a letter on that bitch. How she gonna fuck with me *and* another nigga? That bitch is not gonna play with my heart like that. I know Arnold better have some answers for me. She can't even look at me. I done lost my damn appetite. After drinking my watered down orange juice, I headed out the door. There was no way in hell I was gonna lay back down.
    After count, they busted the doors for us to come out of our cells. When I spotted Arnold in the hallway, I asked the officer in the control booth to let me out so I could get some paper.

Arnold saw me coming and she sped off. She tried to lock herself in the bathroom, but I snatched the door open and pushed her back.

"Help ... help ... he's trying to kill me ... help!" Arnold screamed.

The case manager and sergeants ran out of their offices. A code seven was called (assault on an officer). Arnold started fighting and scratching me. I backed up out of the bathroom as officers came out of nowhere. They grabbed me in a chokehold, picked me up, and slammed me on my head. I went out for a minute. When I opened my eyes, I was being lifted off the floor in handcuffs that had cut into my wrists.

The officers dragged me to lock up. Once they got me in a blind spot so the camera can't see, a big black sergeant with muscles punched me in my eye! It swelled up instantly the size of an egg. I lifted my head and spit on him. Another black officer hit me from the blindside in my temple. I fell over into a corner. They picked me up, dragged me to the hole, and threw me in a room with a steel bunk, which was missing the mattress. I was so confused. Somebody gonna die for this shit!

Every hour, the officers came into my room, asking had I calmed down. Before I could answer, they would walk off.

Five hours later, I was asked to come to the door. I could only see out of one eye, and the whole side of my face was swollen. I stepped out of the cell. Two officers slid the thinnest mattress into the room that I've ever seen. The sheets and blankets appeared to have been pissed on. I walked back into the cell. The officer opened the trap door, and I put my hands through to have the cuffs removed. I snatched my hands back after they took my handcuffs off, thinking that they may try something. They closed the trap door and walked off. I dropped down on the mattress in defeat then lay back and looked at the ceiling.

Johnny

My pops always told me that you could never hold a good man down. I've been to physical therapy for the last two weeks, and I can bend my left leg now. I still got the cast on my left arm, but I'm making progress. Every day that I wake up, I think about killing that nigga Man. J-Money got the blood of a hustler. To be young, my little man held it down. He even opened up another spot in Rocky Mount. They're making two times as much as the other spots, and they're trained to go. J-Money and I are going to check out my nigga, Majestic, in Roanoke Rapids so we can open up another spot.

Hold on! I know that ain't Lil' T going over to Towns' house! Oh shit, that's Lil' T! What the fuck is he doing over there? I got to go see this lawyer and drop some money off in the safe deposit box. This money is getting too much to hide. Two more years and I'm done. I know y'all are like, quit now, you're rich, but enough is never enough. I broke down and bought Jean a car. She's so old school. She wanted a red '78 Mustang. That's her dream car, so I had her one restored. I think she loves that car more than me. Let me stop.

Yo, Towns and little T are coming out of the house together. She got on a gray catsuit and black heels, with a black purse in her hand. This nigga just opened the door for her. Come on, man! She doesn't look her age dressed up like that. I know that pussy is sitting out there!

"What are you looking out the window at?" Jean asked.

I shut the blind. "Nothing, have you seen Towns lately?"

"No, she don't come out like she used to, why?"

"No reason." I laughed

"What's funny?" Jean asked, putting her hands on her hips.

"I think Towns is feeling Lil' T."

"Jason's friend Lil' T?"

"Yeah!"

"Get the fuck out of here!"

"I just saw them leave together."

We started laughing.

I peeped through the blinds again to check on the two shooters sitting in the truck watching our house. I keep shooters around at all times now. Niggas won't catch me slipping like that again. Damn, Jean ass looking good in them stretch pants. I haven't had no pussy in three weeks. I got to try her ass before Jason get here. I pulled out my dick and began to stroke it. Jean had her back turned, looking in the refrigerator. It felt so good stroking my dick.

Jean turned around and jumped like I had scared her. Her big eyes and chocolate face focused on my dick. She put a grape in her mouth and bit it. I could've sworn she pushed nut out of my dick! It shot into the air and landed on the floor. I kept stroking it, making the rest of my cum run down on my dick. I stared Jean in the eyes as I kept stroking my dick slowly.

Jean

Johnny know he's hurt! Why did he want to do this to my pussy? I'm gonna give him what he wants, though. I unbuttoned my pants, turned around, and pulled them down my legs. With a smile, I bent all the way over in front of him so he could see the pinkness between my clit and my pussy hole. Damn, he stroking that big dick! I backed all the way up to the couch, between his legs. My bare foot stepped in his cum. I didn't even care because I felt his dick opening my pussy hole. What a feeling to have a dick open your pussy up to the max. I slid down on his dick head and moved up and down, round and round, to get my pussy wetter.

"Oh shit, it feels so good," I moaned

I slid down a little further, taking five inches into my pussy. Damn, I could feel that fat dick rubbing against my walls. Three weeks without this …

"Damn baby, I'm coming!" I purred.

I lifted all the way up and let my cum drip out of my pussy onto his dick. I couldn't wait any longer, I got to have him back in there! I slid down about seven inches and rode him slow, squeezing my pussy muscles every time I came up. Damn, that's my spot!

I can't help it, I gotta have him a little deeper. Now he's ten inches deep in my pussy! I could feel his dick head rubbing my ovaries. I sped up, but my legs wouldn't stop trembling.

"Ride this dick, girl!" Johnny said through clenched teeth.

I bent all the way over and touched the floor so he could see his dick going in and out.

"Oh John … neeeeeeee …"

We both came at the same time and foamed around his dick. Oh my, he's trying to push it all in me! I did a slow wine on his dick as he pushed as far as he could go up in me.

In minutes, my cum was running down his dick again. He gripped my ass and exploded deep in my pussy. I lifted off Johnny's dick, turned around, grabbed his dick with both hands, and licked it like a big ass candy cane. Johnny laid his head back on the couch. *Let me stop before he wants some more. With that big ass dick, he got to let the pussy rest,* I thought.

Oh fuck, I heard some loud music. I ran to the window and peeped out. It was Jason! I put my pants back on and grabbed my grapes off the table. Johnny put his dick up and went to get something to clean the stain off the floor. I acted like I was watching TV. If Johnny only knew the shit that I used to do in front of Jason, he'd probably kill me. I only did it 'cause I thought he was gay. I wanted to show him what a man is supposed to do to a woman. He learned though. I be hearing him and Keba's little nasty ass in his bedroom.

Chapter 21

Man

Six Months Later

I'm still in the fucking hole. They shipped me to supermax at Polk Institution in Raleigh, North Carolina. These motherfuckers back here are crazy! The damn officers are crazy too. The people at the last camp gave me a street charge for attempted assault and rape of a government official. It ain't nothing my lawyer can't handle. The good thing is, I'm back online. I got a phone! I may have to stay back here until I go home, but I'm going to make the best of this shit.

I tried to call Officer Arnold, but all her numbers are changed. I got something for her ass, though. First, I'm going to handle this bitch ass Johnny once and for all. Niggas tell me he still in the same spot. He thinks he can't be touched with two fucking niggas guarding his crib. My homeboy next door turned me on to a killer on the south side of Tarboro, from a neighborhood called Double L. Money is no problem. I want them motherfuckers to die in a bloodbath. They crossed the wrong fucking nigga! This killer nigga charging me an arm and a leg, so he better put in some major work.

That bitch, Towns, won't answer her phone either. I know she got my messages, but her time will come. Officer Stanley still answers the phone for me and play in that pussy. I don't have no use for her except for phone sex. She still don't know I'm the one that set her ass up. I know y'all don't like me! Fuck it, somebody got to be the bad guy. Shit, if it was all good guys, the world would be a fucked up place, wouldn't it?

I'm sitting here looking at this little nigga on Facebook, Shyleek Almighty. He's eighteen years old with deep waves and eyes shaped like he's Chinese. This pretty boy ass nigga. He told me he done checked out all the areas and sat cars in places. I want to see what this young nigga is made of. Shit, he told me I don't gotta pay until the first body drops.

I'm back, Johnny!

Chapter 22

Arkeba

Today is my birthday! First, let me tell y'all what my baby, Jason, bought me. He bought me another ring. Not that the price matters, but he paid $15,000 for this one. I thought that was it, but he took me to the mall and said I could get anything I wanted. Ten thousand was my limit. I went crazy in the mall. Some of the shit I can't even pronounce. He took me to Massage World to get a massage, then to get my hair, nails, and feet done. He sat with me the whole time. Ain't he sweet y'all? Finally, he took me to his house and sexed me. I had to relieve some stress; he had not given me any in a minute.

I'm greedy when it comes to dick. If I had to choose between that and food, I'd probably starve to death. My baby gave me two nuts, and I still wanted some more. I don't know what is wrong with me. I guess the apple don't fall far from the tree. I love Jason, though. That's my baby!

By the time we got through, it was dark. On my way home to take a shower, Tracy called and asked me to ride with her to the club. I had never been to the club, so I had to get a taste of that life. I called Jason to see if he wanted to go.

"What's good, baby?" he asked in a serious tone.

"I'm going to the club with Tracy, do you want to go with us? You don't have to ride with us, you can follow us so I'll have a ride home. You know how Tracy be wanting to fuck."

"Yeah, I know how y'all be wanting to fuck. I'm going over some numbers with Pops so we can open another store in Fayetteville. You go ahead, and take the camcorder."

"I love you, baby."

"Always and forever."

Soon as I hung up the phone, I ran to the bathroom to shower. I can't believe Grandma told me that I can stay over Tracy's house tonight. She said, "I know y'all are going to party. I used to be young." Shit, that mean that I didn't have to hide it.

After lotioning up, I put on my brown, black, and white Versace dress, no panties and bra needed. My alligator sandals and the ring that Jason had just bought me completed the look. I let my hair hang down my back.

Oh! I got another package in the mail with no return address. I didn't want to open it in front of Grandma, 'cause I didn't know what would be in there, but she wouldn't leave the room until I opened it. It was a check for $20,000 and a gold ankle bracelet with little diamonds.

Tracy pulled up and blew the horn. I grabbed my purse, which matched my dress, my camcorder and headed out the door. Tracy's daddy had bought her a new white Maxima.

"Girl, let's drive your car! You got a new 740 BMW and don't like to drive it."

"Let's go," I said and hopped out of Tracy's car.

We got in my newly shined up car, thanks to Jason's friend, Lil' T's detail shop.

Tracy and I decided to go to Club Boatride in Rocky Mount. The club was packed. We parked and got in line to go in. Tracy was fly too. She wore a Louie white skirt, lime green top, and lime green Louboutins. The heat hit us as soon as we made it through the double doors. They were partying up in there! This shit blew my mind. Tracy grabbed my arm and pulled me through the crowd. My ass was grabbed ten times before we got to the other side where people were standing. I gave this guy $20.00 to buy Tracy and me two strawberry daiquiris, and $20.00 if he brings it back.

Fifteen minutes later, he returned with two cups of a blue drink and gave me my change. I tried to hand him the $20.00, but he refused it. I looked him over; he wasn't bad. Light skinned with a close haircut and a little hair over his lip and under his chin. He wore a white tee shirt, brown desert storm fatigues, and high top white and brown Pumas.

"You good, shorty. Shit, I'm only eighteen myself. I had to get somebody to get that shit for me. They didn't have any daiquiris, so I got y'all the blue motorcycle. My name is Decey, what's up with your girl?"

I sipped my drink then looked over at Tracy. She was sipping her drink out of a straw and holding her pussy as she danced. I burst out laughing.

"Go see. She's good people," I said.

Before he could walk off, this guy walked past me and looked me up and down. I knew him from somewhere. Grabbing Decey's arm, I pulled him back.

"Do you know him?" I asked over the music, pointing to the guy walking through the club.

"Yeah, that's the homie, Shyleek."

"I know him from Double L. Tell him I said to come over here, please."

"Tell her to give me a lap dance when I get back," Decey said and pointed to Tracy.

I watched as Decey whispered in Shyleek's ear and they both looked my way. Shyleek wore a cream Roc Nation button up, blue Roc Nation jeans, cream and red hiking Timbs, and a pinky ring that glittered with diamonds. This nigga made my pussy wet by looking at me. The closer he got to me, the wetter my pussy became.

"What's up?" Shyleek said.

"You're from Double L, right?" I asked.

"Til' my casket drop."

"I used to ride through and see you over Lil' D's house. Why I never see you in school?"

"I don't do European schools. I got my diploma on the internet in six months, and I have a bachelor's in psychology. I'm only eighteen, and I was homeschooled by my moms. I'm sorry, my name is Shyleek." He smiled.

I stood there watching him with my mouth wide open. His country accent and intelligence did something to me. "I … I'm Arkeba," I said and shook his hand. "So what are you doing now?" I asked.

"For now, I'm stacking paper so I can start this digital design business."

"I like your swag, but I have a boyfriend. You can get some of this cake, though, but on one condition."

"What's that?"

"I gotta record us."

"I'll do that on one condition."

"What?"

"I get to fuck you how ever I want to."

Damn, he just made me cum.

"Let's get out of here then!"

"I'm down."

I damn near ran and got Tracy. She was giving Decey a lap dance. I pulled her up and dragged her through the club. When I looked back, she had Decey's hand, pulling him behind her, and Shyleek followed him.

The night air hit us in the face soon as we stepped out of the club.

"Let me go get my car," Shyleek said.

Tracy and I got in my car and waited for them. Shyleek pulled up beside my car, driving a 2006 emerald green Jaguar. I followed him to the Comfort Inn. They must've known they were gonna get some pussy. These niggas already had rooms. We got out of the cars, and Tracy and Decey headed down the hall to their room.

Before we went into our room, Shyleek turned around and stared in my eyes. "However I want it, right?"

I shook my head up and down. Shyleek opened the door and I went in the room first. He took the camcorder out of my hand and closed the door.

Holding the camcorder up to his face, he pressed record and said, "Take off your clothes for me."

Shit, he ain't said nothing. I pulled my dress over my head and stood there in only my sandals.

"Turn around for the camera." I turned around. "Bend all the way over and show the camera that pussy and asshole."

I spread my cheeks open. He walked closer, reached between my legs, and slid his middle finger into my pussy. It made that wet noise. He moved his finger in and out of my pussy from the back. The louder I moaned, the harder he fingered me. I felt myself about to cum. I threw my ass back to his finger. My moans got louder as I came on his finger. He rubbed the tip of his finger on my asshole, letting the tip slip in, then pulled it out.

"Get on the bed doggy style, so your ass and feet will be at the foot of the bed," Shyleek said, taking off his clothes.

I was under his spell and did everything he said.

Shyleek set the camera on the table, pointed at my ass. He pulled a chair to the foot of the bed, sat down, and slid his tongue into my pussy. Shyleek moved his tongue around in circles, touching my walls. He moved in and out of my pussy with his tongue. His tongue slid out of my pussy, and … oh my God! This nigga put his tongue in my ass! He is so fuckin' nasty.

"Oh shit … cummin' … again!" I yelled.

Shyleek slid his middle finger in my pussy as he tongue fucked my ass. Damn, this fucking boy! Now it feels like I'm cumming out of both holes.

Shyleek pulled out of both holes, making me drop to the bed. I heard him open a condom. I raised my ass up, reached back, and made sure the condom was on. His dick was big and fat. I ran my hand back and forth on his dick. He had about nine inches. I put the head at my pussy entrance. He didn't wait. Shyleek pushed all of it in and started pounding my pussy. I threw it back at first, but damn, he didn't slow up.

"I'm ... cumin' ... again!" I screamed as I pulled at the sheets.

I came all over the condom as he kept pounding my pussy. Shyleek slowed down, pulled out, flipped me over on my back, went in my pussy and pushed my legs back to my chest. He pounded my pussy again. I screamed, moaned, cursed and might have said a prayer.

Shyleek pulled out of my pussy, went down, and put my clit in his mouth. As he sucked on my clit, he slid two fingers into my pussy. He pulled his hand out of my pussy fast and pushed the tip of his middle finger in my ass. Cum shot out of my pussy, and onto his arm. Shyleek pulled his finger out of my ass and slid his dick back into my pussy. It wet his condom like a rain forest. He moved in circles in my pussy, then slid out. My pussy felt so empty. He had replaced his dick with two of his fingers. Damn ... what the fuck? I felt something at my ass. Shyleek pushed his dick head in my ass while he continued to move his fingers in my pussy. Damn, my pussy felt so good, but my ass hurt. He fucked my pussy hard with his fingers as he pushed a little more into my ass. I'm coming again! It ran down his finger and dripped on his dick.

After a little more pushing, Shyleek got the whole thing in my ass. He moved in and out slowly. Damn, he's rolling my clit between his fingers. He's speeding up on my ass!

"Shit ... get ... get ... oh ... get it. I'm cumming!"

Soon as my cum came down, he pulled out of my ass, pulled the condom off, and came all over my stomach. I lay back on the bed breathing hard. Shyleek went to the bathroom, washed up, and came back out. I watched him open another condom.

"Round Two!" Shyleek said, smiling.

This boy fucked and licked me in so many positions. I woke up with both of us laying on our side in the 69 position, with his dick on my lips. The battery had died in the camcorder.

I hopped up, rubbed my hair down and stared at this nigga until he woke up and caught me. I put on my clothes and called Tracy's number. She answered the phone in mid-moan.

"Bitch, you better come on before I leave your ass!"

"Oh ... oh ... kay!"

Five minutes later, Tracy was knocking at my door with her heels in hand. I left my number for Shyleek to call me.

Before I got home, my phone beeped with a picture message. I told Tracy to check it since I was driving.

"Girl, it's a dick!" Tracy laughed.

"Whose dick?"

"Shyleek's!" Tracy said, licking her lips. "Can I get some of that?"

"Yeah. I hope our man is at home," I said, trying to get that good dick out of my mind by reminding myself of Jason.

"You don't sound too sure about that."

"Don't put words in my mouth. Girl, how about I let Shyleek fuck me in the ass?"

"I'm not ready for that. Did it hurt?"

"At first it did, but once it got wet, it felt like I was in another world. Let's go buy a strap on so I can do you!"

"Bitch, you crazy!" We laughed. "Girl, wasn't that Lil' T that just passed?"

"It looked like him."

I pulled into my driveway and parked beside Tracy's car. Jason's car was already gone. I knew he picked up and dropped off work at the spots on the weekends, so I didn't really expect him to be there.

Shyleek

I left Decey at the room asleep. I already knew where Keba lived, but I had to find out where Tracy lived. I may need her. Soon as Keba closed the room door, I was right behind her. She didn't even see me. I got in my car and followed them. They were headed toward Keba's house. I saw one of Johnny's workers, Lil'T, ride past me. I swung around and followed his ass. I set my .45 on my lap. Lil'T was headed to the country. I got behind him and flagged him down. He knew my face from the Double L, so he pulled over. We rolled down our windows almost at the same time.

I lifted my gun up fast and shot him in the face. He fell over in his seat. I jumped out and ran to his car. To make sure that he was dead, I put seven more bullets in his head, ran back to my car, and pulled off.

I dialed the nigga, Man's, number.

"Hello," he answered in a whisper.

"Check the papers tomorrow, and send my money in cash to the P.O. Box number that I gave you," I said.

"Who did you make happy?"

"One of the main ones that help run one of their spots. Once you see his name, you'll know who he is and who his dad is." I hung up.

Damn, y'all, that chick, Keba, got some good pussy, but it's all in the game. If we would've met on other terms, I would take her from Jason. But I turned her ass out, so she'll be back. For the time being, I'm going to swing around here to see if I can catch that nigga's daddy coming out of the crib and going to check on his son. His head will be so messed up, he'll never see me coming.

I parked down the road from Tiny's house, got out, and ran back to his house and hid in the bushes. Tiny soon came running out. I stepped behind Tiny and shot him in his upper body seven times. I ran down the street to my car and drove off. It doesn't pay sometimes to stay in the country, a house every half mile. I drove down the road about another half mile, broke my gun down, and threw it out the window in different directions.

I picked up my phone and texted Man. *Your friend Tiny is gone*

This nigga, Man, got some bread. I'm charging him $10,000.00 a body. He's paying $40,000 upfront. Two more bodies and he gotta fill the tank back up. Damn, I still got the smell of Arkeba's pussy on my lips.

Jason

My phone started to ring as I pulled into my driveway.
"Hello!" I answered.
"Yo, what the fuck!" Mouse cried.
"What's good, bruh?"
"Tiny and Lil' T got bodied!"
"What?"
"They found Lil' T down the road from the spot shot up. I guess someone had called Tiny. He was coming out of the house to go check on Lil' T, and they caught him slipping."

Tears ran down my face. I jumped out of my car, ran into the house, and headed straight for my mama's room. Johnny and Ma lay in bed naked. Johnny jumped up with his gun pointed at me.

"Lil' T and Tiny got murdered!" I cried.

Johnny jumped up, put his pants and shirt on, and slipped on a pair of Gucci loafers. I hadn't seen Johnny move like that since he had been shot. My mama lay there looking at the ceiling with her hand over her mouth. Johnny ran out of the room, with me behind him.

We rode in silence almost the whole way to Pinetops.

"I know I should've told you!" Johnny said, hitting his casted arm on the dashboard.

"Told me what?" I wiped my eyes.

"Lil'T is your uncle!"

"How?"

"Him and I have the same daddy. When Pops died, I was in prison, so I asked Tiny to look out for him."

"That's your baby brother, Da?"

"Yeah, he called Tiny his daddy because Tiny raised him from a baby."

"Where is his mama?"

"She died giving birth to him. I let my little brother down!"

"Who's behind this?" I asked, pulling in at the spot.

"I don't know, but I have an idea."

"Yeah, me too!"

"Somebody got to die for this!"

"And they will!"

Grandma Towns

I know y'all are still hating on me! Don't hate me, hate this good pussy! My baby usually call me when he gets home. I wonder why he hasn't called yet. Yeah, that young dick got me gone. I swear him and Johnny must be some kin. He knows how to handle this pussy. I already miss that big dick, and he just left. I thought he would call me before I lay down.

Keba came in the house with a camcorder this morning. I know she has been up to no good because she went straight to the bathroom. Shit, I used to do it to my mama, Cassandra did it to me, and my mama probably did it to her mama. Go straight to the bathroom to get the fuck smell off. As long as she keeps making those good grades, I won't fuck with her. Colleges are calling the house already. My baby gonna do something with her life. Speaking of the devil, why is she knocking on my door like that? I rushed to the door and unlocked it.

"Girl, what the hell you knocking like that for?"

"Lil'T, Jason's friend, and his daddy were murdered a few minutes ago!"

"How do you know?" I asked as I dialed Lil'T's number.

Lil'T's phone went straight to voicemail. I began to cry. Keba looked at me like 'what are you doing?' I kept dialing Lil'T's number over and over, listening to his voice until it said the voicemail was full.

"Grandma, what's wrong?" Keba asked.

"Lil'T can't have left me like that!" I cried.

"What are you talking about?" Arkeba said.

"He left me, Keba!" I cried, still dialing his number.

Arkeba didn't ask any questions. She just held me until I stopped crying and calmed down a little. Arkeba went into the kitchen and came back with a cup of coffee for me. I set it on the table and grabbed the Grey Goose bottle that Lil'T and I had been drinking on.

"It's too earl —"

"Let me get some alone time, Keba," I said, cutting her off.

Keba walked out of my room and closed the door. I grabbed Lil'T's shirt, held it to my chest as I balled up on my bed and cried myself to sleep.

Keba

Oh my God! Grandma and Lil'T! That's where he was coming from this morning. That's why he used to say, 'Hey grand baby,' when he saw me. It would be funny if he wouldn't have been murdered. Damn, I forgot to text Jason back. He said something about they killed his uncle, Lil'T, and Tiny. I knew he needed me.

I got dressed in a white button up Gucci shirt that came to my knees, a brown Gucci belt around my waist, and brown Gucci heels. My pussy and ass were still sore from last night! I gotta get this nigga out of my mind. Every time I close my legs, it aches and makes me think of him. Even when I took a shit, I thought about him.

On my way out the door, Tracy called my phone, asking about Lil'T and his daddy.

"Girl, it's all over the news!" Tracy said.

"I'm going where Jason is right now."

"Tell him if he needs me to do anything, I'm a phone call away."

"Alright, remind me that I got something to tell you later."

"Okay, bye."

I pulled up at the spot in Pinetops. The yard was full of Johnny's workers and gunmen. Jason saw me pull up and walked to my car. He got in on the passenger side and closed the door. I kissed his lips and hugged him tight.

"Bae, are you all right?" I asked.

"They killed them, Keba!" Tears rolled down his face as he stared straight ahead in a daze. "We got a meeting with Pops, I'll talk to you later."

"Call me if you need me," I said and kissed him again before he got out the car.

I was stressed out, and fully awake. There was no way I was going back to sleep. I went against my better judgment and called Shyleek. He answered the phone in a sleepy voice.

"I'm sorry, did I wake you?" I asked.

"Yeah, what's good?"

"My boyfriend's friend and his dad were murdered this morning."

"Damn, cupcake, sorry to hear that. What can I do for you?"

"Can you sex me slow this morning, so I can ease the stress?"

"Come on, baby."

"I'm turning in now."

"Okay."

Shyleek had the door cracked when I got to it. He met me at the door, took my clothes off, and kissed me from my forehead to my toes, then turned me around and did the same thing. My sore pussy felt like it had a heartbeat in it.

"No recorder this time?" he asked, guiding me to the bed.

"No, not this time."

Chapter 23

Jason

Johnny paced back and forth in front of his little homies. "I don't know who is responsible, but I will close every drug spot that I own if y'all don't find out who did this," Johnny said as he paced. "I don't want to see any more of y'all hurt or dead. Somebody out there is catching us slipping. We know it's someone that we know or have seen before, because whoever shot Lil'T pulled him over, or he had car trouble. We all knew how Lil'T was about that car. Do any of you know where he was coming from?"

Johnny looked at all of them, but no one said a word. Once he turned his head away, they looked at each other.

"Y'all can go, let me speak to my son," Johnny said.

"What's good, Pops?" I said after everyone had walked to their cars.

"One minute I'm Johnny, and the next Pops. Go check the CO chick out and see if she has heard from him."

"I'm on it," I said.

"Listen, Jason, in this game, there will be more losses than ever. That's why I stay on you about going to school. I want revenge as much as you do, but you can't show people your feelings and weak spots in this game, either. We show that only when we catch the motherfucker that done it. When people see what can hurt you or cause you pain, they'll know how to come at you. Tighten up."

I walked to my car, thinking about what Johnny had said. The whole ride to Officer Arnold's house that Jay-Z song played in my head. Lil' T used to play it all the time. "When I die, don't cry my niggas/bust shots in the sky, my niggas."

I didn't even know if this chick had found out that I lied to her about Man. Fuck it, if she calls the police, I got enough money to beat the case. I knocked on the door.

Someone looked out of the peephole and stood there. I heard Arnold say, "Hold on," then I heard what sounded like running away from the door.

I was about to take off running to my car when Arnold opened the door in a cropped tank top that showed her stomach, pink khaki shorts, with Snoopy bedroom shoes on.

"You came to finish me off?" she asked.

"No, I came to check on you. See? No skirt or hair bows."

Arnold stepped to the side and let me in.

I walked into her home with my hand on the handle of my gun, which was tucked under my shirt.

"No one is here. I live by myself, so I walk around nude. I had to go put some clothes on," she said, embarrassed.

I still looked around, paranoid. Damn, her ass done got plump. She turned and caught me looking at her ass. Arnold had a trail of hair on her stomach, going down into her shorts.

"Do you want something? Cause if you don't, I would—"

"I didn't think you would recognize me," I said, cutting her off.

"How could I forget them eyes? You were getting ready to cut my baby out!"

"I'm sorry, I really am a good guy."

"Prove it."

"What do I have to do?"

"Order us a pizza, no pork, and watch this movie I just ordered. It should come on in an hour."

Arnold gave me the number to order the pizza, and I called and placed an order. I took my two chains off and set them on the table, holding my gun at the same time. I asked this chick what I had to do to prove to her that I'm sorry. She wants to eat pizza and watch a movie. Shit, I would've taken her out to eat and took her shopping, even bought her a new car if she wanted it. I really was sorry for what I had done. I had to do what I had to do, though. I forgot she didn't know how long my money is.

I looked out the window and saw a black Navigator sitting across from Arnold's house. I knew Johnny had them niggas following me. I had peeped them in my rearview mirror on the way over here.

"Don't worry, no one is coming over here," she said, causing me to close the blind.

"Ain't no men chasing you?"

"No, since my abortion, I've been single and staying in the house."

"Do you still work?"

"No, I've been looking for a job. I might have to move, I'm tired of my mama and daddy paying my bills."

Damn, I fucked shorty's life up!

"Did you go to college?"

"Yes, I went to college for business management, with a concentration in international business."

"My mama is looking for someone to manage her Jamaican club and restaurant. She has one in Rocky Mount and one in Raleigh."

"That's your mama? She's so fly! Where did she get her style?"

"Just know that she's spoiled."

Arnold smiled.

Damn, I got her to smile.

"I've been to her club in Raleigh twice."

"I'll tell her to give you a call."

The pizza man rang the doorbell, and when Arnold got up, I couldn't help looking at her ass. I paid for the pizza. We had twenty minutes to burn.

"So has that crazy man contacted you?"

"I haven't heard from him in a minute, and I got all my numbers changed."

"What's a minute?"

"Since he tried to attack me at the prison about six and a half months ago."

She ran the story down to me. Arnold really thought Man was trying to kill her. I got to take this one with me to my grave.

"Damn, shorty."

"That's not my name, and my last name is Arnold."

"You never offered your name."

"You never asked."

"I'm asking now."

"My name is Sanatra Arnold. The movie is about to start."

Sanatra went into the kitchen and came out with two paper plates and two cups of Kool-Aid. She put two slices of pizza on both plates. I stared at the Kool-Aid and she caught me looking. Sanatra drank from both cups, then gave me her cup.

"Satisfied now?"

"Yeah." I tasted the Kool-Aid. "This is good."

The movie was old school, *Barber Shop 2*. As it started, she left and came back with a small bag of strawberry dro.

"You smoke?" she asked.

"Every now and then. Did you keep that pound he told me to get from you?"

"I still got it, really. I only smoked an ounce of it in six months."

Sanatra rolled the blunt and lit it. She coughed a little after two pulls, then passed it to me. I pulled that shit one time. It damn near killed me! I started coughing and could not stop. Sanatra had to go get me some water. The cigarillo went out in the process. I took her lighter off the table and lit the shit back up. She burst out laughing. I hit it softer two more times and passed it back to her. As we watched the movie, everything was funny to our high asses. By the time the movie went off, the pizza was gone, and so was all the Kool-Aid.

"Sanatra, I want to sex you good, but I got a girl."

"Well, if you got a girl, then you don't need me."

"We have sex with other people, we just let whoever we have sex with know what time it is."

"I don't want to be a part of that right now. I'll call you if I change my mind."

"I guess that means it's time to go?"

"Yes, thanks for the company. Call me, my number is 827-4288."

I programmed her number in my phone, then gave her mine. Sanatra got up, put my chains around my neck, and walked me to the door. I turned to tell her bye and she kissed me on the lips.

When I stepped out into the sun, the Navigator was still there. I got into my car and took off. The truck followed.

Keba

My whole body ached as Shyleek walked me to my car. I can't believe that nigga sexed me like that. He got my cake swollen. I can't even close my legs all the way. I'm not gonna kiss him goodbye because then I'm not going to want to leave. I shut my car door and drove off. He watched me until I turned the corner. As I drove home, a song by New Edition came on the radio. The lyrics seemed to speak directly to me. "You can't have your cake and eat it too, girl. Between me and him, you got to choose, girl."

I'm not choosing anyone. My man is Jason.

I walked slowly to the house after I pulled into my driveway. I felt Grandma's hurt as soon as I opened the door. Lil' T must have torn that stuff up. Grandma sat on the couch, looking at a picture on her phone. I didn't know what to say. I rubbed her back, then went to the bathroom to soak. After running my water, I eased down in the bubble bath, just as my phone rang. Jason's name was on the caller ID. I spilled water all over the floor, answering his call.

"Come over here and wear those crotchless panties I bought you."

"Not right now, bae. I'm in the tub."

"Word, that's what's up."

"I'll call you after I get out of the tub."

"Alright, bae."

"Love you."

"Love you too."

I felt so bad that I couldn't give my baby no cake. I dialed Tracy's number, and she answered on the fourth ring.

"Girl, turn that shit down!" I said, trying to hear her over the loud music.

"What's up, baby?"

"I'm sore, and Jason want some cake, but I can't give him none right now."

"That nigga tore that cake up, didn't he?"

"I went back and got some more."

"Girl, you is something else. I'll be through there."

"Alright, thank you."

"That's our man. We're supposed to be there for him."

"Okay, bye."

"What did you have to tell me?"

"Call me, I'll tell you tonight. I'm going to sleep," I said and hung up.

Jason

Arkeba is tripping! I'm over here high and horny, and she's talking about not right now. I went to my room and turned on the PlayStation 2. Just as I was about to put Mortal Kombat: Armageddon in, the doorbell rang. I went to the door, and Tracy stood there in a DKNY jumper and sandals, with her hair hanging down her back. I took my camcorder off the table and hit record.

"Who's here?" Tracy asked.

"Nobody, but me."

I put the camcorder on its stand and pointed it toward us. Tracy unsnapped her jumper and it fell to the floor. She was naked, except for a half t-shirt. Tracy pulled the t-shirt over her head. Her breasts pointed right at me. I put her nipple in my mouth and rubbed between her pussy slit. Her bald pussy was soaking wet. I wanted to be in that pussy right then! I took a condom out of my pocket, dropped my pants, and rolled it on. Pulling Tracy close to me, I turned her around and bent her over the arm of the couch. I got on my knees and put hickey marks all over her ass cheeks before I spread them and licked her pussy from the back.

The smell of her vanilla body lotion made me want her more. I put her cake lips in my mouth and sucked on them, then licked from her clit to her pussy hole, over and over. Cum ran out of her pussy onto my tongue. I stood up with her cum shining around my mouth and slid my dick all the way in her pussy. It was a perfect fit.

Tracy threw her ass back to my dick, and I felt myself about to cum. I took the condom off and Tracy turned around and took my dick in her mouth. She looked up at me as she sucked and jacked my dick at the same time.

"Yo ... yo ... Tra ... oh ... fuck!" I came in her mouth.

I looked down at Tracy, and she kept sucking. My dick got back hard instantly. She let my dick go, sat on the couch, and put her legs behind her head. I stood there with my mouth open, looking at her fat clit. Tracy reached down and opened her pussy lips as I rolled on another condom. I squatted down in front of her and slid my dick in her pussy. She moaned loud as I pounded her insides.

The weed had me ready! I kept pounding her pussy. She screamed like she was cumming. I stopped and went in circles while Tracy reached down and rubbed her clit.

"Oh ... I'm cumming!" she screamed.

Tracy

Damn, he's tearing me up! What has got into him? I thought about Keba letting Shyleek fuck her in her ass and pulled Jason's dick out of my pussy. Taking a deep breath, I led it to my asshole. He had to push hard several times before his head popped in.

"Damn ... that ... shit ... hurt!" I yelled.

Rubbing my pussy in circles, I pushed two fingers in.

"Oh ... shit ... it ... hurt," I said as he tried to push more in.

I took my hand out of my pussy and pushed back on his chest so he couldn't go all the way in.

"Shit ... girl ... shit!" Jason said, with his eyes closed.

That shit turned me on. I moved my hand and Jason sank deep in my ass. I thought to myself, *Keba wasn't lying.*

Jason fucked me slow. "Damn ... so tight and good!" he whispered.

Oh shit! He's moaning about how good it is. My ass got even wetter.

"Get that ass, boy. Get it!" I yelled.

Jason did it faster and harder, and I screamed my ass off. He pulled out of my ass, took the condom off, and went back in my pussy.

Oh my God! I never felt the meat before. I came just from feeling him without a condom.

Jason pulled out of my pussy, grabbed the camcorder, pulled me up, and led me to his room. He set the camcorder facing his bed. I lay in the middle of Jason's bed, fingering myself. He lay down beside me. I climbed on top and rubbed my pussy all over his dick, then slid down and licked my cum off him. I turned with my back facing him, grabbed his dick, and put it in my pussy. I leaned over as Jason spread my cheeks apart and slid his finger in my ass.

"Damn it ... damn it!" I moaned.

I felt myself cumming. My pussy tightened as my cum ran down Jason's dick. I turned back around and bounced on his dick as he squeezed my nipples. It felt so good. I bounced harder and faster until Jason rolled me over and pushed my legs back to my shoulders and fucked me hard.

"What's wrong with you?" I screamed, but he kept pounding away.

I tried to slide away from him, but Jason pulled out of my pussy, turned me back on my stomach, and went back in my ass. I reached back and spread my ass cheeks. That must have turned him on because he fucked my ass harder. That shit hurt, but it felt so right. Finally, I felt myself cumming as Jason lay on top of me.

"Damn, baby. Damn, girl!" Jason moaned in my ear.

I felt something warm go up my ass, and I came right behind him. He slid out of my ass and went to wash off. I was half asleep when Jason got on top of me missionary style and pushed his dick deep into my pussy while he sucked on my bottom lip. He moved in circles in and out of me. I moved with him as I came again.

"I love you!" I yelled as he sped up in my pussy.

Jason pulled out and came all over my pussy lips. I lay there with my eyes closed, moaning as I rubbed his cum on my pussy lips. He got up and went to the bathroom. A few seconds later, I heard the shower running. Jason came back and led me by my hand to the shower, then he went back to get the camcorder.

He washed me from head to toe with the soapy sponge. I turned around so he could wash my back, and he pushed me against the wall and put that fat dick back in my pussy. Jason fucked me from the back slowly, then he slid back out of my pussy, finished washing me off, and carried me back to the bed.

Damn, Keba, we got us a beast!

Shyleek

Damn, Tracy is over Jason's house. I just called Arkeba, and her grandmother said that she was asleep. It sounded like she was crying. I think Arkeba, Jason and Tracy got some other shit going on. I headed to check out his mother at the Jamaican restaurant. That's a sexy ass old lady. I gotta try to get in her head so I can get to Johnny.

I hoped she was there, as I got out of my car and went inside. The place stayed packed. Damn, I can't believe that she's right in front of me. Look at that ass! She was wearing a white with red pinstriped Vera Wang business suit, and white open toe Louboutins. She wore her dreads in a wrap. That accent made me want her so bad. When she walked over to my table, I looked at her dark face and licked my lips.

"Sir, I'm Jean, someone will be with you shortly. Would you like something to drink and rolls while you wait?"

I stared at her breasts. "I'll take two of them.

"Stop playing," she said and laughed. "Would you like something to drink?"

"I'll take a Ting and you."

"Bwoy, you are crazy. One Ting coming up." She smiled as she walked off.

Jean's walk was just right. Her ass jiggled with each step. I bet she doesn't even wear panties. A young Jamaican girl came and took my order. I like Jamaican women; they play hard to get. After eating jerk chicken, cabbage, rice and peas, with a side of plantains, it was time to go. These niggas need to make me think a little harder. I'm going to knock off some more of Johnny's workers. Grabbing the plastic gloves off the counter as I walked out, I wondered if the white '88 Buick Regal was still there.

Nas and Damien Marley blasted from my stereo system all the way back to Tarboro. I had already scoped these niggas out, so I parked my car across the street from where I'd parked the stolen hooptie earlier. I got into the car, put the plastic gloves on, along with my rasta hat with the fake dreads attached, and tied a t-shirt around my face, so only my eyes showed. I lifted the back seat and pulled the AK-47 out.

After I hotwired the hooptie, I drove around the corner. Three guys stood in front of Johnny's spot talking. I grabbed the AK from the passenger seat, aimed it out the window, and let that thang sing on their asses. They tried to reach for their guns, but it was too late. I gave them niggas the business and pulled off. The police don't be on this side of town, so I knew it would take them a while to get there. Instead of flying out of the hood, while reloading my gun, I circled the block.

Just like I thought, them niggas had their backs turned, tending to their homies. I stopped in the middle of the road and chopped down them two niggas helping the dead. I still drove off at a normal speed. Instead of going all the way out of their hood, I parked the car in the same spot, took the disguise off, and put it in the book bag. I put my fitted hat back on, got out, and walked back around to the scene of the crime. On my way, I dropped the book bag in a trash can. Police were everywhere. They were looking for a dread driving the Regal, with a green, red, and yellow rasta cap on.

I listened to an old lady tell me what happened before I walked back to my car across the street and pulled off. I picked up the phone and texted Man.

You owe me $50,000 more.

Jason

I awoke to Tracy lying on my chest and my phone ringing.

"Please get that," Tracy said. "It's been ringing off the hook."

I hopped up and grabbed my phone.

"Hello!" I snapped.

"Bruh, somebody came through and shot the spot up. Bobo, Trap, Bookie, and Aaron are dead!" Mouse said sadly.

"Where were you when it happened?" I asked as I wiped my tears.

"We heard shots and looked outside. Bookie, Bobo, and Aaron were laid out in front of the house. I was in the spot getting the stuff packed before the police came!"

"Do you know who it was?"

"No, but when I came outside, he had doubled back. I wasn't strapped, so when I saw him coming back with the gun, I dropped to the ground. I guess he thought he had hit me too. I've seen them eyes before somewhere."

"What eyes?"

"It's a certain look to his eyes that makes him stand out."

Tracy came in the front room and sat down next to me. I remembered what Pops said about showing my feelings, and I tried to fix my face.

"I'll talk to you later," I told Mouse and hung up.

"What's wrong, Jason?" Tracy asked.

"Four of my homies just got killed!"

"Damn, that's six in one day!"

"My pops is gonna flip!"

"I'm going to tell Keba!"

Tracy put her clothes on, rubbed my back and walked next door to Keba's house.

I got up and paced the floor. What in the hell was going on? I didn't even know who to kill. I dialed Johnny's private number.

"Hello," he whispered. "I'm in a meeting."

"Pops!" I said in a sad tone.

"What's wrong, J-Money?"

"Bobo, Trap, Bookie, and Aaron were killed today!"

"How?"

"Somebody did a drive-by on them!"

"How did Trap get shot? He's supposed to be in the house."

"They heard the gunshots and ran outside to help Bobo, Bookie, and Aaron."

"That still don't explain how Trap got shot."

"Whoever it was doubled back and shot again."

"What kind of shit is that?"

"I don't know, Pops," I said in a sad tone.

"Let me guess, don't nobody know nothing."

"Mouse claims his eyes look familiar, but he can't place him."

"This shit is getting crazier by the minute."

"I know," I said, choking up.

"What I tell you about that shit?" Johnny said and hung up.

I didn't even hear Arkeba and Tracy come into the house, but when I looked up, they were standing over me.

"Are you all right, baby?" Keba asked.

"No, but I'm gonna be all right."

I stood up and put my boxers and pants on. "I gotta make a quick run. Y'all gonna stay here?" I asked.

"No, we'll be over my crib," Arkeba said.

Keba and Tracy walked out of the house, but Tracy ran back inside and took the disk out of the recorder.

"I gotta look at this. I'll bring it back," Tracy said.

"Make sure that you do," I said and reached for my ringing phone.

"Ms. Mary around the corner said she watched a guy throw something in her trash can. She said she thought it was some money, so she waited until the police left and went to check. It was a rasta cap with fake dreads attached, and a dingy white t-shirt," Mouse stated.

"And?"

"That's what the shooter had on when he came through. I'm trying to picture this nigga with a short cut, now. Bruh, I don't forget no faces. I know I've seen them eyes before."

"Alright, hit me if you remember."

"One."

I had to do something to occupy my mind. Sanatra popped into my thoughts, and I dialed my mama's number.

"Hello," she answered.

"I called to see if you're okay. It's a lot of crazy stuff going on around here."

"I heard what happened. I'm on my way home now. I gotta get up early to go check on the club."

"Have you found someone to run the club yet?"

"No, I'm doing everything."

"My friend girl has a business degree, and she is looking for a job. Give her a call."

"Text her number to my phone."

I left the house looking both ways, with my gun out. The guards sat in the truck, but I had to make sure I was good myself.

The gunmen followed me to the spot. Johnny was holding another meeting, and he didn't even tell me. I wonder what that's all about. After he finished talking, everyone left. They looked in all directions, with their hands on the butt of their guns. Johnny pulled me to the side.

"What are you doing here?" he asked.

"Why shouldn't I be here?"

"Whoever is doing this is trying to destroy me or get at me. I don't want them to get at you, to get back at me. You're the only blood I have left."

"I'll fall back some, but when I find out who did this, they're gonna wish they were dead before I kill them!"

I got into my car and drove away.

Arkeba

Tracy and I sat down and watched both tapes of us getting fucked by Jason and Shyleek. I can't believe that Jason put it on her like that. He never gave it to me like that. I'm heated with him, though! He fucked Tracy without a condom. He and I never fuck other people without a condom.

Tracy got up slowly. Damn, Jason fucked the shit out of her. He better be ready to give me some tomorrow. I still think Shyleek put it down harder, though. I gotta leave this nigga alone; he's fucking with my head. Tracy kissed me on the lips and got ready to go.

"Bye bitch," I said, slapping her on the ass at the door.

"Girl, don't do that! I'm going to soak my body!" Tracy said as she got into her car.

Grandma came out of the room with a t-shirt in her hand and the phone. She really was taking Lil' T's death hard. I didn't know what to say to my grandmother about the death of her eighteen-year-old lover, or whatever y'all want to call it, but I had to check on her.

"Grandma, are you all right?"

"They killed my baby! He made me so happy." She started to cry.

Damn, Grandma loved that boy. I didn't even know about them. I probably would've cursed Lil' T's ass out. I'm gonna miss his crazy ass, though. I wiped a tear from my eye. My grandmother needed me more. I went over and hugged her tight. She leaned on my shoulder and let her tears go.

As I comforted my grandma, I wondered if Shyleek had another chick at the room.

Man

The Next Day

My little nigga go hard! I laid the newspaper down and smiled. Hold up! I picked the paper back up and read it. The paper stated that it was six people, not seven killed. Let me call this lil nigga.

"Hello," Shyleek answered.

"What's good, player?" I asked.

"Let's get something straight. We're not friends, I'm a working man for those that can afford me."

"Lil nigga, I don't care about all that! I called to tell you that you missed one."

"What the fuck are you talking about?"

"The paper says six people were happy, and I paid you for seven."

"It'll be taken care of, but I gotta let shit calm down first."

"Just start with the main people I want. They deserve to be happy."

What the fuck? I looked at my phone. This lil nigga hung up on me. I think I'ma have to teach his ass some manners when I get out of here. He's a damn baby to me, and he's gonna show me some respect. Thinking of babies, I wondered if Sanatra had our baby. If she killed our baby, I'm going to kill her ass. I also wondered what Towns fat pussy ass is doing. She still won't answer the phone, but she'll come around. She always does.

Chapter 24

Tracy

Two Months Later

Damn, what am I going to do? I'm two months pregnant. I don't want to lose Jason and Arkeba. They mean so much to me. I've been fucking crying for two damn weeks. I'm all cried out. I'm supposed to go to college next year. Fuck it, either they're going to ride with me or they're not. I gotta talk to Jason about this first. Keba is my friend, but it's me and Jason's baby.

I took baby steps toward my car. This shit is not gonna be easy. I dialed Jason's number as I got into my car.

"Where are you?" I asked when he answered the phone.

"I'm at the crib, about to go check on this new watch store that we're opening in Virginia. You want to go with me?"

"I need to talk to you, could you wait for me there?"

"Yeah, bae, I'll be here."

I drove to Jason's house in a daze. When I pulled in his driveway, two men came from the sides of the house with assault rifles. They scared the shit out of me. When the gunmen saw that it was me, they stepped back behind the house. I almost ran inside. Mouse sat at the kitchen table in front of a skinny nerdy looking white guy describing someone, as the white man drew on a piece of paper.

I went to Jason's room and found him sitting on a leather couch in a Sean John business suit, brown alligator dress shoes, and an all-white Sean John button up with no tie.

"How are you gonna ask me to go with you, and I'm dressed like this?" I had on a white tee, black jogging pants, and my Dora the Explorer bedroom shoes.

"So what? I take my two ladies as they are."

"Would you take me if I was pregnant?" I blurted out with tears in my eyes.

Jason looked me in my face, then at my stomach. He sat there quiet. His silence was killing me.

"So how far along are you?" Jason asked.

"I'm two months."

"So, am I …"

"You're the only one I've been with in my life without a condom. If those guys' condoms didn't bust, or they didn't do no grimy shit, then it's yours."

"Your mama know?"

"Yeah, she told my dad and he blanked. They gave me the decision to have it or not."

"Whatever you decide to do, I'm with you. But if you decide to have it, no more different partners while you're pregnant. So get used to Keba's pussy, her toys, and me."

"I love y'all, Jason," I cried.

"We love you too. Come here and stop that crying." He pulled me to him and held me in his arms. It was the best feeling I'd had in two months. "Talk to Keba about it. I'll see y'all when I get back."

"Is she home?"

"No, she left with some guy in her car earlier."

Shit, I can about narrow that down to her and Shyleek. I looked at Jason to see if he was tripping about it.

"Who was the guy?" I asked.

"I don't know. You know how y'all love dick."

Jason pulled me up and guided me to the front room. Johnny held up two pictures of a guy with half his face covered. He had slanted eyes, a small nose, and thick eyebrows, with dreads. The other picture was of him with a close haircut.

"Do y'all recognize his face?" Johnny asked.

Damn, I know those eyes from somewhere. My mind just couldn't find a face to fit them.

"No, I don't know him. Who is that?" I asked.

"The guy that killed some of our homies is this guy or favors him," Johnny said, holding the pictures up.

Jason took the pictures out of Johnny's hand. He stared at the pictures and gave them back to Johnny.

"Naw, I don't know that nigga."

Jason walked out the door behind me, rubbing my ass. No sex in two months, he better stop! I turned around, grabbed his dick, and tongued him down. When I let go, his dick was sticking straight out. Jason watched me get in my car before he got into his car and drove away.

I dialed Keba's number.

"Hello," Keba moaned.

"I need to talk to you."

"Come to the Red Roof Inn in Rocky Mount, room 215. Boy … stopppp!" she yelled and hung up.

Keba had my pussy wetting the seat of my jogging pants.

I made it to Rocky Mount in ten minutes and rode around until I spotted Keba's car. I got out, took a deep breath, then released. I don't know how she's going to react to me telling her this. The ride on the elevator seemed to take forever. After I got off, my walk to their room felt like a lifetime. When I knocked on the door, Keba peeped out and opened it in some boy shorts and a bra. The sex smell made my body tingle as I walked in the room. Shyleek lay on the bed, staring at me lustfully.

"What's wrong, baby?" Keba asked.

I covered my stomach like I was protecting my baby.

"I need to talk to you in private," I said, cutting my eyes at Shyleek.

"My bad, I gotta use the bathroom anyway," Shyleek said and went into the bathroom.

I pulled the hotel chair over and sat in front of Keba. I grabbed her hand and looked into her eyes. "I'm pregnant!" I whispered.

Her eyes grew big. "Why wasn't you using condoms?" Keba whispered.

"I was. I only went one time without a condom."

Arkeba stared at me then pulled her hand away. I guess she thought about the video she had seen of Jason and me.

"Is it Jason's?"

"I think so."

"Have you spoken to him?" I shook my head yes. "So you talk to him before you come to me?" she said with an attitude.

"It's not like that and you know it." I began to cry.

She wiped my tears away. "Stop crying. I know you, and I know you've cried for many days behind this. If Jason is cool with it, then we are having a baby."

"Thank you, I love you!" I began to cry again.

"Stop crying and take those clothes off, so I can show Shyleek how I like my pussy ate," Keba said, taking off her boy shorts and bra.

Keba grabbed my pussy. I squeezed my legs together, closed my eyes, and bit my bottom lip. Keba pulled my shirt over my head. I stood up and stepped out of my jogging pants. She kissed all over my stomach. Every kiss she planted seemed to make my wetness drip out of my pussy onto the floor. I climbed on the bed and opened my legs wide. Keba climbed between my legs, opened my pussy lips, and called Shyleek's name. He came out of the bathroom with his shirt over his nose and mouth.

"Don't nobody go in there for about ten or fifteen minutes!" Shyleek said, sounding like Ice Cube's daddy on Friday.

Keba burst out laughing. I stared at him, stuck for words. It's him! He's the one on the drawing that Johnny had! Oh my God, he's walking toward me.

"Oh ... oh shit!" Keba pushed two fingers into my pussy.

I had to play it off. I moaned when Keba licked my clit. Damn, it's been so long y'all. I'm scared and horny.

"Oh ... oh ... oh!"

Keba licked my pussy slit from my hole to my clit. She did it over and over, tickling my clit with the tip of her tongue and moving the tip of her finger in circles inside my pussy. Her finger was soaked.

"I'm ... fuck ... cumming!" I screamed as Keba kept licking until she had devoured all of my cum.

I slid away from Keba. She had her eyes closed and was cumming too, as Shyleek ate her from the back. I slid off the bed, barely catching my balance.

"Where are you going?" Shyleek asked, causing Keba to open her eyes.

"What's wrong now?" Keba asked.

"Nothing, I have to go," I said.

I put my clothes on and headed for the door. When I opened the door and looked back, Shyleek was fucking Keba from the back. She moaned my name as I closed the door behind me. Soon as the door closed, I took off running with my Dora the Explorer bedroom shoes in my hand. I got to the car and called Keba's phone. She didn't answer. In tears, I sat there for fifteen minutes, trying to decide what to do. I gotta tell her what's good, but I can't tell her around him. She may panic, and he might hurt her. I began to cry. I have to call Grandma Towns.

"Hello," she answered sadly.

"Grandma Towns, I need you to call Keba right now and make her come home, please!" I cried.

"What's the matter?"

"Her life may be in danger."

"Okay, I'll call now."

"You can't tell her that her life may be in danger because she might panic, and the person she is with might kill her."

"I'll sit here until she comes out!"

"Look, I'll call her on three way, and you tell her that you came here and police are everywhere."

I sat and waited until Grandma Towns clicked back over to me.

"Hello," Arkeba answered.

"Oh my God, your grandma, Keba! Come home, police are everywhere!" I screamed and hung up.

Arkeba

I hopped off the bed. "Put your clothes on, we have to go!" I yelled to Shyleek as I stepped into my jeans.

"What's wrong?" Shyleek asked as he put his clothes on.

"My grandma needs me," I cried.

I ran out the room with Shyleek behind me. We took the side stairs and ran to my car. As I took off out of the parking lot, I told him what Tracy had told me. The whole ride back home, I cried, praying that she was all right.

After I dropped Shyleek off in front of Double L, I raced home. It only took a few minutes, but it seemed like hours. I pulled into my driveway, almost hitting Grandma's car. I didn't see any police or yellow tape. I let out a long deep breath of nervous air. Tracy turned into the driveway behind me and got out.

"What's going on, Tracy?" Grandma asked, walking out of the house.

"Yeah, what's going on, Tracy?" I asked with an attitude.

Did she understand my grandmama is all that I have left? How can she play with me like that?

"Grandma Towns, let me talk to Keba, then we'll explain."

Grandma walked on the porch, sat down, and watched us. I crossed my arms and stared at Tracy. This better be good, or I'm going to punch this bitch in the face.

"Shyleek is the one that's been killing Johnny's little homies," Tracy said.

"Bitch, go ahead with that bullshit. You know he doesn't move like that!"

"Listen, Keba!" Tracy almost yelled. "When I went to talk to Jason about me being pregnant, Johnny had Mouse sitting at the kitchen table with a white man in front of him, drawing the person who did the drive-by shootings. They were done when I came out of Jason's room. Johnny held up two pictures and asked me if I knew the guy. I couldn't place him because he had dreads in one picture, and a close cut in the other, with a shirt covering his face. I told Johnny I didn't know who he was, which at the time, I didn't. I knew them eyes looked familiar, though. So, when I saw Shyleek come out of the bathroom with his face covered, I knew it was him!"

"I don't believe it, and if you're gonna be on some fuck shit like that, maybe we shouldn't be friends anymore!" I said and walked into the house.

This bitch is tripping for real. I never hated on her, even after she got pregnant by Jason. Why is she gonna hate on me with Shyleek? I got deep feelings for that boy. She better gone with the bullshit. I flopped down on the couch. I could see out the screen door that Tracy's car was still outside. I hope she doesn't tell Grandma that shit, and I really hope she doesn't tell Jason. If it was true, he probably would kill my ass this time. Let me call this bitch and tell her not to go lying to Jason. I dialed her number, but she did not answer. I looked out the window and saw Tracy walking over to Jason's house. The two gunmen stepped from the side of the house. Jason walked to the door and handed her some papers.

I saw Tracy take the papers and walk back to my house. As she was walking up the steps, I opened the door to blank on her ass. She held the picture up to my face. I stood there, staring at the image. My hand went to my mouth. I back stepped, turned and ran to my room.

Before I could shut my door, Tracy was pushing it open. Grandma watched us, shaking her head. Tracy pushed her way into the room and closed the door. I sat on the bed. Tracy stared at me with her arms folded over her stomach. I jumped up and started packing.

"What are you doing?" Tracy asked.

"I'm getting the fuck away from here. When Johnny finds out about this, he's gonna kill me!" I cried.

"Stop it, Keba!" Tracy said, snatching my clothes out the bag as fast as I put them in.

"I've put his family in danger before. He won't forgive me this time."

I couldn't be strong anymore. I dropped to the floor.

"We gotta tell Grandma Towns."

"What if he's the one that killed Lil' T? She will never forgive me."

"Why would she not forgive you because of that?"

"I forgot to tell you. Grandma and Lil' T were fucking."

"What?" she yelled.

"Don't say anything, Tracy, 'cause when people mention his name, she ends up crying."

"Damn, they were like that?"

"What am I going to do?"

"We gotta tell Grandma Towns."

"Y'all don't gotta tell me shit, I heard it all!" Grandma busted in my room with her hands on her hips. "See what your pussy done got you into? I told y'all little hoes to wait until you are married. I guess the apple don't fall too far from the tree," she said and lit her joint.

"I didn't know!" I cried.

"I'm gonna fix this when you go to school tomorrow. Call him and tell him to come over here tomorrow morning after I go to work."

"I'm not gonna put you in danger!" Keba said.

"Bitch, you already have! If Jason kills you, do you really think he's gonna let me live?" she said, and I started to cry. "There's no need to cry now, you wasn't crying when he was in that pussy!"

Grandma hit her joint and handed me the phone. I dialed Shyleek's number with trembling hands.

"Yo," he answered.

"Hey baby, what are you doing?"

"Is your grandmother all right?"

"Yeah, she had a reaction to some food."

"I was just thinking about you."

"I hope it was about how you love being in this cake."

"You already know it. I miss it already."

"My grandmama go to work in the morning. Come give me some."

"I'll be over there."

"Okay, bye."

"Peace."

Y'all know he couldn't turn this pussy down! When I hung up, Grandma turned and walked out of the room. I lay back on the bed and thought about how niggas keep tricking me, and how I keep putting people's lives in danger. Tears rolled down my face. Tracy wiped my tears away as her phone rang.

She put the phone on speaker. "Hello."

"Why didn't you tell me I was gonna be a granddaddy?" Johnny asked.

"I was waiting for Jason to tell y'all."

"Maybe that baby will slow y'all down some."

"It will, believe me."

"Did Keba know that face?"

"No, I'll take it back over there."
"Keep it, we got copies."
"Alright, bye."

I lay on the bed staring at the pictures of Shyleek. I wanted it not to be him so bad. Tracy's mama texted her to pick up her cousin from football practice, so she kissed my chapped lips and left.

Grandma turned on her CD by DRS, and "Gangsta Lean" came through the speakers.

I knew she was thinking about Lil'T.

Chapter 25

Shyleek

The Next Morning

Man had texted me three names that weren't on my list, but hey, the customer is always right. Besides, he has offered me double for this one. I looked at my watch. I gotta hurry up and handle my business. It was 7:30 A.M., too early for me to be up.

I stepped out of the stolen Honda Accord in front of the baby mansion. I wore a Duke University hat pulled low, a Duke sweater, acid washed jeans, and black Docker sneakers, with the backpack on my back. I rang the doorbell.

A white woman appeared at the door in a black Liz Claiborne business suit. She looked to be in her forties, slender with shoulder length hair and brown eyes.

"I'm sorry to bother you this early, is your husband home?" I asked.

"Yes, he's getting out of the shower. Please come in," she said.

The woman walked away from the door to the front room. She had a nice ass to be a snow bunny. The lady turned and caught me looking at her ass. She blushed. I took the backpack off and set it between my legs.

"Nice house y'all have here. Only you and him live here?" I asked.

"Yes, I think we've waited too late to have kids."

Chuck walked down the stairs in his robe. "Who are you?" he asked.

"Man sent me." I smiled and pulled the .22 out of my backpack.

They both put their hands in the air.

"Whatever he's paying you, I'll double it. And, I have thirty bricks of coke in the back of my store."

"Like father, like son, right?"

"I had no choice but to sell coke. It was passed down from my father. Either I did it or they would kill me!"

Chuck threw the store keys to me. "The key to the safe is there also, just leave us alone!"

His wife sat there crying, shaking out of control. I looked at my watch. Damn, I want to fuck his wife, but I gotta go. I put the gun to the front of Chuck's head and pulled the trigger. He crumbled to the floor and his body began to jump.

Chuck's wife stood frozen in shock for a minute, then she turned to run up the stairs. I aimed at her head and hit her in the shoulder. She kept running, holding her shoulder. The second bullet hit her in the back of the neck. I ran upstairs and found her on the floor, holding her throat. I aimed the gun at her head and pulled the trigger.

I ran back downstairs and saw that Chuck had slid to the phone. I watched him dial 911, then shot him in the back of his head. He slumped to the floor in a puddle of blood.

I put my backpack on and walked out of the house. As I drove out of the neighborhood, police cars sped past me. Damn, they got here quick! I drove the car downtown and parked it in a courthouse parking lot beside my car. I took the Duke hat and sweater off and put it in my backpack, then I got into my car with the backpack and drove off. I'll hit the jewelry store up when shit cools off. Arkeba, you got some good pussy, but your name is on the list too, baby. I got to hit that one more time first, though.

Grandma Towns

What's taking this motherfucker so long? I might as well light one up to calm my nerves. I lit my joint as I heard a car pull up. Looking out the window, I saw Shymeek, Shyleek, whatever his damn name is, getting out of a brand new Jaguar. Somebody got some damn money. I understand why Keba let him do all of that freaky shit to her. Yeah, I snuck into her room again and saw the CD. I thought she was on drugs. I guess that dick was her drug.

I told Keba to drive my car to school today, so he'll think she was still there. Before he could knock, I pulled the door open. He stood there with his mouth wide open, looking me up and down. His eyes stopped at my pussy print. I wore a pair of Keba's small jogging pants. They were tight and pulled up between my pussy lips. My breasts almost spilled out of my tank top.

"I'm sorry. I have —"

"Nigga, stop lying. Keba don't hide shit from me. She decided to go to school because I stayed home," I said, cutting him off.

I'm gonna call him Shy, 'cause I forgot the damn boy's name. Anyway, Shy still stared at my pussy print.

"You got some weed?" I asked.

He just stood there staring.

"Boy, do you have any weed, yes or no?" I demanded.

"Yeah, I got a little bit in the car."

I watched him go to the car and come back to the door. He thought I didn't see him slide something under his seat. I walked away from the door so he could come in."

"Here you go, ma'am," he said, walking into the house.

"Roll that shit up," I said.

Shy broke a cigarillo open and rolled the weed up. I sat in front of him with my legs wide open. His eyes kept dropping to my pussy print. The seam of the jogging pants sat between my pussy lips like a thong. Shy hit the cigarillo two times and passed it. I hit that shit and went into a coughing fit. I forgot you can't hit this kind of shit hard. I hit it soft and didn't cough, but the shit had my pussy jumping.

"Let me see your dick," I said.

He looked up in shock. The weed actually made him look Chinese. Damn, this young nigga is making my pussy wet.

"Say what?" he asked.

"Let me see your dick!"

He looked between my legs and saw that my moisture had seeped through my jogging pants. His dick stood straight up. Shy unzipped his pants and pulled his dick out. Nine inches ain't bad at all, and it's fat!

"Jack it for me."

Shy stroked his dick while I stood up and rolled the jogging pants down my legs, then pulled the tank top off. I stood naked in front of him. He stopped and stared at my pussy. Shy stood up and removed his pants and boxers, then sat back down. I stood over him, pulled my pussy lips open, and sat down slowly on his dick. I moved up and down, with my eyes shut tight. Damn, this young motherfucker got some good ass dick! I see why Keba couldn't believe that he killed those boys. The dick was too good to let go. I bounced up and down on his dick. He closed his eyes as I squeezed my pussy muscles, making him bite his bottom lip.

"I can't believe it ... I can't believe it!" Shy moaned, rubbing my pussy lips every time I came down. I tried not to cum, but this boy ...

It was so much cum that his dick hairs were drenched. I felt him about to cum. He grabbed my hips and pulled me down on his dick. I had to fight it. I hopped up off his dick before he came. Shy leaned back in the chair with his dick sticking straight up, breathing hard. My cum shined on his dick like a fresh paint job. I walked in my room and stuck my head back out the door.

"Are you coming?" I asked.

Shyleek smiled. Damn, this nigga is fine. He walked into my

room with his dick hard and swinging. BOOM! I shot him in the chest with my double barrel shotgun. He flew back out of the room and landed on the living room floor. There was no need to check and see if he was dead. Them slugs knocked two holes in his chest the size of saucers. The floor was full of blood already. I put my tank top on and a pair of shorts as I heard footsteps running toward my house. I looked out the window. Johnny and two of his soldiers stood there. I opened the door and stepped out.

"Are you all right? We heard a gunshot," Johnny said with his gun in his hand.

I walked up close on him. My pussy lips rubbed against his dick.

"The nigga y'all been looking for is in there dead!" I whispered.

Johnny walked past me with his gun drawn. He saw the guy lying on the floor in a puddle of blood. Johnny looked back at one of his shooters and told him to go get one of the drawings. Johnny watched me leave the room and come back with the drawing that Keba had. He pulled Shy's shirt over his face, put the picture beside it, then looked at me.

"Don't go asking me a lot of damn questions. Just get this motherfucker out of here so I can clean up before my grandbaby gets home! And don't say anything to her or Jason about this!"

Johnny stood and watched the gunmen clean up.

An hour later, the body was gone, and everything was cleaned up. Just as I was about to light a joint, Arkeba and Tracy ran in the house early from school.

"Did he come, Grandma?" Keba asked.

"No, I got up before he got his nut!" I burst out laughing.

"Grandma, this isn't a laughing matter!" Keba said.

"Just know you'll never get any more of that dick!" I laughed again. "You better take this to your grave, 'cause I'm not saving your ass anymore. And keep your legs closed!"

Chapter 26

Arkeba

One Year Later

I rubbed my stomach as I walked across the stage to get my diploma. One more month and this baby will be out of me. Jason's horny ass had knocked me up. I heard my grandma, Johnny, and Jean screaming my name and cheering. My grandma stopped when a white man in a business suit approached her. I thought for sure it was a detective. As I took my seat, I saw Grandma point to me.

I watched Tracy walk across the stage and get her diploma. Her mother and father clapped and screamed. Her son, Lil' J, clapped his hands too. Then, Jason's name was called. We all screamed and clapped for him. I got up to take pictures with some friends when the white man who was talking to Grandma approached me.

"Arkeba Towns?" he asked.

"Yes, that's me."

He handed me an envelope with my name typed on it. "We've been looking for you for about ten months. Your father and his wife were murdered a year ago. They left no other family but you. One man called, claiming to be his brother, but he's not listed in any of the wills. You're a very wealthy young lady. Here's my card. Come by the office Monday morning so we can get the papers signed."

Jason and Tracy walked up after the man left, and I explained what it was about. Jason, Johnny, and Jean were already rich and had quit the game. Jean owned three restaurants and two clubs. Jason and Johnny owned five watch phone stores, and Jason had reached out to someone in LA, and he is about to start his own porn company. With Grandma's permission and a piece of the pie, Jason had sold the tapes of Grandma, Mama, and me to Vivid Entertainment for two million dollars and a distribution deal for his company. The porn movies of us hit stores and shot through the roof. They were called, *The Apple Tree*.

Johnny, Jean, and Jason moved into a baby mansion behind the mall. Jason bought me and Grandma a big house right next door. Y'all know he wasn't going to leave me over there. Tracy's family still didn't quite understand our relationship, but most of the time, she's at my house anyway.

Jason

We did it, y'all! Now it's time to stack even more legal money. The girl with the big ass that I hit in the school bathroom, Carla, called Keba, Tracy, and I to take a picture. As we posed for the shot, I noticed Johnny pulling everyone back so the gray-haired man in his electric wheelchair could get by. He held his head down, coughing as he rolled in front of them. My family was all smiles as they watched us.

All of a sudden, the old man jumped from the wheelchair and pulled an Uzi from under his suit jacket. He sprayed my mama, Johnny, and Grandma Towns. People ran in all directions.

I spotted the man running through the crowd. His wig had blown off. As I ran behind him, he turned to shoot me. That's when I recognized him. It was Man! A policeman fired a shot, dropping

Man to the ground. The gun flew out of his hand. Police surrounded him with their guns pointed. Man saw me standing there staring at him, and he burst out laughing.

I ran back to where my mama, Johnny, and Grandma Towns lay in puddles of blood. Johnny was hit the worst. He had pushed my mama and Grandma Towns to the ground. They were still hit, though. The paramedics were loading them onto stretchers as Keba and Tracy cried hysterically. Once they were in the ambulance, we ran to the car and took off for the hospital. Arkeba lay in the back seat screaming and crying. Tracy climbed back there to hold her. I drove the best I could, but I don't know how I made it to the hospital in one piece.

At the hospital, Keba, Tracy, and I sat and waited. An old white man sat across from us. He was at least sixty years old, on the short side, with white hair.

"Can I see you in the hall for a moment?" he asked me.

I followed him into the hallway, and he turned to face me with an angry look.

"Call me tomorrow, it's very important," he said and handed me a card with just a number on it.

Before I could respond, he walked away. I wasn't thinking about shit he was talking about. My only concern was my family. After surgery, my mama and Grandma Towns were moved into a room. Pops was still in surgery. About an hour later, the doctor came out of the operating room.

"He made it through surgery," the doctor said. "It's up to him, now."

I thanked the doctor and went to see my mama.

Arkeba

Man has four policemen guarding his room door. I wish I could get in there with that motherfucker. Grandma's room was across from Man's room. Grandma was asleep when I went into her room.

I sat in the chair beside her bed, rubbed her hand, and pushed her hair behind her ear, as my tears dripped onto her sheets. I stood up fast. Them police are gonna let me get to Man. I don't care what they say! An envelope dropped out of my pocket. I picked it up and looked at it. I'd forgotten that the white man had given it to me at the graduation. I flopped down on the chair, wiped my eyes, and opened the letter.

Arkeba,

Baby, I'm sorry I wasn't in your life, but as you know, I'm white, and I was married. I didn't want to lose my family. I've always supported you financially. As for your mother, I'm sorry about what happened to her, but she kept blackmailing me for money to get high. I got my brother, Man, to give her the high that she wanted.

Yes, Man is your uncle. He is my daddy's son. I didn't know that Case was Towns' daughter until she was pregnant with you. I tried to get her to abort you, but I'm glad she didn't. Your grandmother, Man, and Johnny robbed and killed my father, your grandfather. I sent you the videos, trying to show you why your grandmother and Johnny were going to die. I guess you're not as smart as I thought you were.

I don't blame Man because he didn't know that was his father. He didn't find out until his aunt made him dress up, took him to a white man's funeral, and told him that it was his father in the casket. I remember it like it was yesterday, because I asked my mother who were those people. So, I forgave my baby brother. In order for me to forgive him, he had to kill Towns and Johnny, and I backed him financially so he wouldn't have to spend any of his money.

I should be old and dead now, so I would like to apologize for all that I've put you through. If I could bring your mama back, I would, but Towns and Johnny, I'll meet their asses in hell. I hope this ten million dollars will make up for all the hurt I caused you. The rest of the money and the store will be left to my wife, and hopefully our kids. We haven't got lucky yet, but when we do, you'll need to meet them. I do love you …

Love Always,
Daddy Chuck

Apple Tree

Tears rolled down my face. I couldn't believe my supposed to be father was responsible for this bullshit. I threw the envelope down, and a tiny picture of a white man fell out. I flipped the picture over, and it said, *To my oldest girl, Daddy loves you.* I dropped the picture on the floor like it was on fire, remembering him from the jewelry store and the funeral. I staggered to my grandmother and grabbed her hand. I laid my head on her chest and cried.

"Grandma, please hurry up and get well. I need you!" I cried.

Chapter 27

Jason

One Month Later

I was happy to see my pops home. Although he has to learn to walk all over again, I'm glad that he is alive. I went to my room and looked out the window. An old white man kissed Grandma Towns on the lips and walked to his car. I wanted to yell out the window at him, but I didn't want to wake Keba and my baby boy. I ran down the stairs to catch up with him, but he was already gone. I remembered that I had left the card he gave me in the car, so I ran to get it. I found it in my sun visor and dialed the number. A recording came on, saying, "The voicemail of the Honorable Judge Moore, leave a message."

I hung up and paced the floor. Five minutes later, I called again. He answered this time.

"Judge Moore speaking."

"I'm Jason Bullock."

"Meet me at seven, in front of your house. My friend wishes to speak with you."

I couldn't wait to see what was going on, but I couldn't trust it as long as Man was still alive. I made some calls to my old homies to have my back.

Around seven, an unmarked patrol car pulled up. I stood there with two guns under my shirt. A tinted window came down. An older white man whom I have never seen before drove the car, and Judge Moore sat on the passenger side.

"Get in," Judge Moore said.

I got in the back seat with my hands on both handles of my guns.

"This is my close friend, he runs the county jail. Man killed his niece and her mother, who is his sister. He wants Man dead," Judge Moore said.

The man looked in the mirror at me and nodded his head.

"You've got one day to do as you like, but make it look clean. The cameras will be down for two days. You have a week from today to make it happen."

Man

A Week Later

That damn Johnny and Towns just won't die. They tricked me into killing my daddy. If that little nigga, Shyleek would have killed Arkeba like he was supposed to, I would be the last one with my father's blood. He fucked my money up! When I find his little bastard ass, I'm gonna kill him! Niggas think they not gonna see me again. I got a lawyer to beat the case. I have so much information on so many dead bodies that I can walk in front of a judge and walk out the same day. Y'all can call me what y'all want, but don't call me collect.

Where the nurse at with my medicine? My back is killing me from that gunshot. I heard some keys; that better be my medication, or I'ma flood this bitch! The white nurse was so scared of me that before she would come in my room, the jailer would make me turn around to get the shot in my back. I'm not going for that shit today.

"Brown, turn around and lift your shirt," a female officer said.

"Fuck no, I want to see who's putting this damn needle in me."

A beautiful nurse walked up with a needle in her hand. All I could do was smile at her. My dick stood straight out.

The nurse looked down at my dick and licked her lips.

I pulled my shirt off, turned all the way around, and backed up to the bars. I felt two needles enter my back.

"Oh shit!" I screamed.

The injection was hot. I ran by my bunk and turned around. The nurse leaned over and kissed the officer on the lips. The woman officer removed her hat and let her hair fall down her back. Goddammit! Under all that thick brown makeup, it was Arkeba.

"Hey, Uncle Man!" Arkeba smiled.

I tried to yell, but no words came out. Blood ran out of my eyes, down my cheeks, and onto my chest. I attempted to lift my hands and wipe the blood away, but my body had locked up. My eyes and ears leaked blood, and I felt something running out of my dick and ass. More blood bubbled out of my mouth in clumps as I fell over to the floor.

A male officer opened the door with a twisted sheet in his hands. He tied one end around my neck and the other end around the light.

Squatting down in front of me, he said, "Pops told me to tell you, scared money don't make no money."

He stood up, walked to the cell door, and looked back at me with a smile as I choked. Then, he grabbed Arkeba's hand and the nurse's hand and walked away.

Damn, they got me …

Epilogue

After selling the store, and all of my daddy and granddaddy's property, I am worth 39 million dollars. I attend the University of North Carolina, and I just opened four stores in big cities that sell sex toys and sexy outfits. I'm studying computer engineering and psychology, and I have an interactive porn website, www.pussyrequest.com where people can virtually direct their own porn scenes. Damn, that made me think about ... never mind. Now where was I?

Johnny and Jean finally got married after Johnny learned how to walk again. He and Jason were now completely legit businessmen with their porn company, the watch company, and several stores. Jean opened three more restaurants, including one in Jamaica. She keeps her grandbabies all the time, and she just found out that she is pregnant.

Jason attends college at N.C. State, majoring in architecture. He just started a clothing line for thick and big women.

Tracy attends the University of North Carolina, studying international business and taking pre-law classes, so she can take her place in the Bullock Family Corporation.

Grandma let a producer at one of the biggest porn distributors in the world take pictures of her pussy and alter it to fit the prettiest porn chicks on the market. Every time they use her pussy, she gets paid big! And, she finally found her a man around her age who can keep up.

Sanatra managed Jean's club for a while, before starting her own marketing firm with Jason's backing. Her client roster is growing by the day. She and Jason have some kind of closeness, but y'all know he's here to stay. That Towns pussy rules.

The apple didn't fall far from the tree.

The Beginning!

Available Now!

Made in the USA
Columbia, SC
18 February 2025